Middle School Blues

Other Avon Camelot Books by
Lou Kassem

A HAUNTING IN WILLIAMSBURG
SNEEZE ON MONDAY

Avon Flare Books

LISTEN FOR RACHEL

Middle School Blues

LOU KASSEM

AN AVON CAMELOT BOOK

AVON BOOKS, INC.
1350 Avenue of the Americas
New York, New York 10019

Copyright © 1986 by Lou Kassem
Published by arrangement with Houghton Mifflin Company
Visit our website at http://www.AvonBooks.com
Library of Congress Catalog Card Number: 85-27092
ISBN: 0-380-70363-7
RL: 4.8

First Avon Camelot Printing: September 1987

CAMELOT TRADEMARK REG. U.S. PAT. OFF. AND IN OTHER COUNTRIES, MARCA REGISTRADA, HECHO EN U.S.A.

Printed in the U.S.A.

OPM 20 19 18 17 16 15 14 13 12

For my husband
who married a square peg
in this round world.

Middle School Blues

1

This is my first funeral. I'm not going to any more. Except my own.

They're doing everything wrong ... the music, the flowers, the long, solemn faces. Gram would hate it and it's her funeral.

I wish they'd asked me what Gram wanted. You'd think her own daughters would know better.

Gram is — was — my father's mother. She was a very "up" person. Instead of playing "Rock of Ages" they should be playing "I've Got a Home in Gloryland." Gram liked music with a beat to it.

And these flowers! Gram hated cut flowers. I can still hear her saying to me, "Don't pick the flowers, Cindy. Let them bloom where everyone passing by can enjoy them."

I wiggle a little on the hard wooden pew. Mom frowns a warning at me.

The heavy scent of flowers is making me sick, but I sit still again and shut my ears to what is going on. I will remember Gram in my own way . . .

Tabitha Jane Tallman Cunningham — Tabby for short — had hardly ever been sick a day in her whole life. I guess she surprised everyone by dying last Thursday. Gram was full of surprises.

When Gramps was alive he used to laugh and say Gram was like an old tabby cat; if you treated her right, she purred, but if you didn't, watch out for her claws! Personally, I never saw any claws on Gram. All I saw was a little, smiling woman in a denim skirt and blue sneakers, who'd let me be myself for one wonderful week every summer. Not that I didn't have to mind or do my chores! There's lots to do on a dairy farm as big as Belle Meade. But Gram never yammered at me to keep clean, act like a lady, or stop asking questions. She never made fun of my schemes even when she knew they wouldn't work.

I remember the time when I really wanted to be a boy. Miss Minnie, a mountain herb doctor who was a friend of Gram's, claimed to know a magic spell that would grant my wish. She told me that if I could say the magic words and kiss my elbow under a full moon, I'd turn right into a boy! I practiced and practiced, almost tying myself in knots — without much success. But I wouldn't give up. Gram never said a word, even when I broke her favorite lamp.

On the last night of the full moon, I went to bed early. I set my alarm for moonrise. It didn't go off,

2

but something woke me about one o'clock. The moon was on the other side of the house so I ran out into the back yard. The rose garden looked so eerie in the moonlight. I said the magic words and tried with all my might to kiss that elbow. I'm not sure what happened next but I know I screamed when I hit the water. I was still sitting in the fish pond watching a goldfish swim around my chest when Gram came flying out in her nightgown.

She looked at me and said, "Well, stand up! Let's see if it worked."

When we saw that it hadn't, she hugged me — wet pj's and all — and said, "Be happy to be yourself, Cindy. I like you just the way you are."

That's the kind of person she was. I'm really going to miss her . . .

Mom nudges me to my feet. The church service is over. Silently we pile into the waiting cars and follow the hearse along the winding road to Mountain View Cemetery.

The family is seated on folding chairs under a big green awning. About half of Albemarle County is standing beside us — the better half, of course. We are an old Virginia family. Cunninghams have lived in the Piedmont since 1740. Dad's one of the few who left the area and didn't take up farming. He's a research scientist for K.D.L. Laboratories. Some folks think he shouldn't have gone, since he was the only son. Gram and Gramps didn't feel that way. Gram told me so . . .

Why is my head running on like this? . . . There's Miss Minnie in her floppy straw hat and flowered dress. People are giving her funny looks, but I'm glad she came to say goodbye to Gram . . .

Pastor Percy is waiting for everyone to settle down. He hasn't been Gram's pastor very long. Gram didn't like him as much as she did Pastor Smythe. Pastor Smythe would roll up his sleeves and help Gram in her flower garden. Pastor Percy wouldn't think of doing that. He might get his hands dirty or mess up his wavy brown hair. Gram said he had his hair styled at her beauty shop! I heard her call him Prissy Percy once . . .

Pastor Percy adjusts his robe, smooths his hair, and clears his throat.

Everyone gets quiet.

A nosy yellow jacket circles Pastor Percy's head as he begins. "For our last farewell to our good friend Tabitha Cunningham I will read her favorite psalm, Psalm 121." He pauses and brushes away the annoying yellow jacket. "I will lift up mine eyes unto the hills, from whence cometh my help (*swipe*). My help cometh from the Lord, which made heaven and earth. He will not suffer thy foot to be moved (*harder swipe*). He that keepeth thee will not slumber . . ."

Miss Minnie is mouthing something and waving to get Pastor Percy's attention but he ignores her and continues. So does the yellow jacket.

"The sun shall not smite thee by day . . ." (*swat! swat!*)

4

I feel a giggle building up and press my lips shut to keep it inside.

Pastor Percy finishes the psalm and begins talking about Gram and Heaven. The yellow jacket lands on his head and begins crawling toward his ear.

What if it goes inside? I can't hold it in. A giggle bubbles out.

"Sh-h-h!" whispers Grace, my older sister.

Mom squeezes my hand so hard my fingers crunch.

Pastor Percy's warmed up now. His voice rolls out deep and mellow like a song. The yellow jacket takes off and whizzes around the pastor's head three times.

What happened next was like one of my Saturday morning cartoons.

The yellow jacket landed on the Bible Pastor Percy had tucked under his arm. With a triumphant look on his face the pastor smacked at the yellow jacket.

At the same moment Miss Minnie screeched, "Don't swat!"

Pastor Percy missed.

The yellow jacket flew up the sleeve of his robe. It must have stung the pastor several times because he was yelping and dancing around like crazy as he tried to get his robe off.

Several people rushed up to help him. I was laughing so hard I fell off my chair.

Mom yanked me up. "Stop that, Cynthia Jane. This isn't funny."

I tried to stop, but when Miss Minnie's voice rose

5

over the clamor saying, "I told him NOT to swat!" my laughter rolled out again.

Grace jerked me out of my chair, marched me to our car, and shoved me inside. She plopped down beside me, silently fuming. Her face looked sunburned.

No one spoke to me all the way back to Belle Meade.

As soon as we got out of the car Mom said, "Go to your room, Cynthia. And don't come out until I tell you to."

I did as I was told. I've been up here for two hours. I still don't see why everyone's so upset. It was funny! I'll bet Gram is laughing — wherever she is.

Most adults take everything so seriously. It's a crime to laugh — especially at funerals.

I only wish Gram hadn't died before I could tell her about my latest plan. I, Cynthia Cunningham, am going to write a book! The idea came to me about two weeks ago. This summer has been the pits. My two best friends went away for the summer. Jeff went to a sports camp and Becca went to visit her grandparents while her folks were in Europe. I had a choice of going to camp or taking private saxophone lessons. I chose the sax lessons. I'm not sorry, but you can't talk to a saxophone! I wound up spending a lot of time at the pool or at the library. Home has been impossible.

My family is a perfectly ordinary, average family. (Middle class, Grace says.) Grace is twenty, tall, blonde, and a junior in college. She inherited Dad's brains. Ellen is eighteen, tall, blonde, and just starting college. She inherited Mom's beauty. Then there's me — twelve, short, brown haired, and not very smart or pretty. In fact, according to my family, I don't look or behave like anyone from either side. I'm a square person in a round family. It's never really bothered me. Mostly we get along pretty well. Until this summer.

Beginning the day after Ellen's high school graduation, our house was in a turmoil. Do you know how many hours of shopping, exchanging, and packing it takes to get two girls ready for college? Plenty! Believe me. It took four trips to the store, two letters, and one phone call to Ellen's new "roomie" just to get the right bedspread!

"We'll never get done in time!" Mom wailed at least once every day.

"I hope you don't wear out your credit cards," Dad would say, laughing. I thought I detected a note of concern behind his laugh, but no one else seemed to.

When they noticed me at all, I got a message loud and clear — TIME FOR A CHANGE. My rough edges must be rounded off. And what miracle was going to accomplish this change? Middle school! Practically every other sentence had those two words.

"Oh, Cindy! A girl in middle school shouldn't have to have bubble gum cut out of her hair *twice* in one week!" Mom said when I won the pool bubble gum championship.

Shoot! Everyone knows once you blow a bubble it has to go somewhere. Besides, I like short hair.

"I was so embarrassed!" Grace moaned when she bandaged my skinned knee and elbow. "Girls in middle school don't climb trees, much less have to be rescued by the Fire Department!"

"I was going after Mrs. Wimmer's cat," I protested.

"Maybe we should have named her Calamity Jane," Dad said. (That's his favorite joke.)

Mom shook her head and said, "There goes another pair of shorts! Throw those in the trash, Cindy. They're beyond repair."

Ellen ruffled my hair, which I hate, and said, "Middle school will change all this."

That and a few hundred other such remarks started me thinking. I went down to the library to find out more about this new thing I was going to experience.

Would you believe they didn't have a single book — not one — about middle school?

Oh, they had books like *Your Baby, Your Three-Year-Old, How to Live with a Teenager, Married Life of the Golden Years,* and *Your Retirement.* But not one book about the in-between years, especially not one about how and what to do if you find yourself stuck in that age.

I felt like Cinderella. One wave of the magic (middle school) wand and I was supposed to turn into a beautiful, well-behaved princess. I tell you they really had me psyched!

That's where I got the idea of writing a book. I'll keep notes as I go through this uncharted maze and then I'll write all about it. Maybe it won't help me, but it might help some other kids like me — if there are any. Dad says I'm one of a kind.

So, while I'm sitting here waiting for my release, I might as well start.

> RULE No. *1: Don't laugh at funerals. Adults don't have a sense of humor like kids do.*

"Cindy, open the door."

It was Mom. I stashed my notebook in the desk and went to turn the old skeleton key. Mom could have opened the door if she'd jiggled it. Gram knew that. She could always get me out if she wanted to.

Mom came in and hugged me. "Cindy, I'm sorry. With all of Gram's friends and neighbors calling, I forgot about you."

I squirmed loose. I guess I was still hurt. Besides, I don't like mushy stuff. "Are you still mad at me?"

"No, Cindy. We know how much you loved Gram. People handle grief differently. You were overwrought. I should have realized that."

"Is Dad still mad?"

"Cindy, I don't even think he noticed. Come on downstairs and eat some dinner. People have brought enough food to last a week."

"I'm not hungry."

"Come on, Cindy," Mom said, giving me a watery smile. "Miss Minnie's here. She's been asking for you."

I went. But only because of Miss Minnie. I may never see her again.

2

"You're as nervous as I am, Becca Morgan." I was bouncing up and down on my bed, trying to see if I could reach the ceiling now that I'd grown one quarter of an inch.

"No, I'm not," Becca replied smugly. She sat cross-legged on the floor watching me.

"Are . . . too!"

"Am not! Mother says it's going to be the happiest time of my life."

"When was the last time your mother was right?" I asked. I flopped down on the bed and looked her straight in the eye.

"I can't remember." Becca giggled.

Mrs. Morgan is a nice lady. She makes great chocolate chip cookies and lousy predictions. "Remember when she said if we kept those frogs we'd have

11

warts? Or when we made faces our faces would freeze that way?"

"Or if we ate all our carrots we could see in the dark?" added Becca.

"Yeah, I remember that one. I fell down two flights of stairs testing it. How about when she said eating our liver would make us pretty? Sheeze! I ate enough to be Miss America. All I got was sick."

"Well, at least you don't have tired blood," Becca said defensively.

"Right!" I agreed. I thought I'd better change the subject. It isn't good manners to criticize your best friend's mother, even if she is wrong. "Are you going to ride the bus tomorrow?"

Becca nodded vigorously. "Mother wanted to drive me but I said it was babyish. She finally gave in."

"Good. I didn't want to ride with Jeff. He's acting very funny."

"When did he get back?"

"Yesterday. It isn't fair! He grew a whole inch and a half this summer." (Jeff is my second-best friend. He lives next door.)

"Boys grow faster than girls," Becca said. "They're even born longer." Becca is full of such tidbits. Her father's a doctor.

"Big deal! My sisters were taller than I am when they were twelve. I can tell by the marks on the kitchen door. At this rate I'll be a midget. And don't say 'Good things come in small packages' or I'll barf!"

Becca looked offended. "I wasn't going to say that. You must have some short genes in your family."

"Sure. Two pair right in my dresser drawer."

Becca looked puzzled. Sometimes she isn't on my wavelength.

"Short jeans . . . like in blue . . ."

We both broke up over it. It felt good to laugh.

Becca wiped the tears from her cheeks. "Honestly, Cindy, how do you think of such things so quickly?"

"I don't know. They just pop into my head and right out my mouth. Ellen says I have a quirky mind."

"Ellen says? Boy, that's rich! All she thinks about is boys, clothes, and college. You said so yourself. Talk about quirky . . . hah!"

Being around Becca always makes me feel better. She's not as pretty as my sisters. But she will be when she gets her braces off. Yet she never makes me feel dumb, awkward, or short.

I grinned. "Yeah, you're right. She's quirky but at least she's lived through middle school."

"I don't see why middle school should be so much different."

"Neither do I. But everyone here expects great changes. They've been on my case all summer. If you'd been here you'd know what I'm talking

13

about," I said, glaring at her. I still hadn't quite forgiven her for her desertion.

"Don't look at me like that, Cindy! You know I didn't have any choice. Besides, I'm back, aren't I?"

I grinned and forgave her. She was right. At our age you don't have many options. "You sure are! And tomorrow we are officially members of Ruffner Middle School, God help us."

"Or them," Mom said, standing in my doorway with a batch of fresh laundry. "Here. Put these away. In your drawers neatly, please. I don't want you to look as if you'd slept in your clothes all summer."

"How could I? Everything's new," I muttered. I had been dragged along on several of those miserable shopping trips. I hadn't outgrown my old clothes. Why did I need to buy new junk?

Mom turned to Becca. "I bet you have lots of new clothes, don't you, Becca?"

Becca blushed. She hated being a traitor, but she had to tell the truth. "Yes, ma'am."

Mom gave me an I-told-you-so look and left us alone.

We goofed around for a while listening to records and stuff, then Becca said she had to go home.

"It's still early. I thought we could round up Jeff and some other kids and play kick-the-can," I said.

"I'd better not. I promised Mother I'd be home early. She wants to use some special rinse on my hair."

"What for?"

"Oh, you know. She wants to bring out my highlights or something," Becca replied, blushing again.

I knew Mrs. Morgan all right. She can hardly wait for Becca to be all grown up. I gave Becca my sternest stare. "She didn't make you buy a bra, did she?"

"No!"

"Okay," I said, relenting. "Our pact still holds! No harnesses until ab-so-lute-ly necessary."

"Right!"

Becca held her pinkie finger next to mine and we curled them in our secret sign. Then she left and I went to find Jeff.

Mrs. Johnson said Jeff had gone with some guys to Games-R-Fun. Personally, I can think of better ways to use my allowance. Feeding quarters to a machine is dumb.

I was pretty hacked at my friends. Here was our last night of freedom and I didn't have any company! For consolation, I practiced my sax for an hour and a half.

When I put my horn away, Grace yelled, "Thank God!" My sisters are definitely not music lovers.

3

Becca missed the bus.

I found out later that the rinse her mother had used turned Becca's hair a bright red. Mrs. Morgan had to wait until the drugstore opened to get another rinse to put Becca's hair back to its original color.

Of course I didn't know this at the time. All I knew was that I didn't have anyone to sit with. Jeff went straight to the back of the bus and sat with the guys. Since I'd never been on a school bus before, I followed him. That's when I noticed something strange. Boys sat in the back. Girls up front.

I walked back up front while the bus driver glared at me in his mirror.

"Find a seat, kid," he snarled. "I can't go anywhere until you're seated."

I flopped into the first seat I came to.

"This seat's saved!"

I moved quickly across the aisle.

The bus lurched forward, dumping my sax and notebooks all over.

"Little seventh grader," someone said. My face felt like I had a fever of 102 degrees.

The bus pulled into the rear of the school. Everyone scattered in all directions. I was mixed up. On orientation day we had gone in the front doors! It took me fifteen minutes to find the auditorium where the new students were meeting. (I also found the gym, the boys' locker room, and the cafeteria in my search.) Ruffner is sure a lot bigger than Meadowbrook.

In the auditorium, I sat down next to a chubby girl who looked almost as upset as I felt. A man who looked like a movie star came on stage and introduced himself as our new principal, Mr. Zale. He said he was new at Ruffner too. We'd learn the ropes together.

The chubby girl sighed loudly.

Mr. Zale gave the same orientation speech we'd heard last spring.

I craned my neck to find Becca or some of the kids I knew from Meadowbrook. I only saw a few. I guess that's not too unusual. There are over two hundred of us from five elementary schools.

Mr. Zale began introducing our teachers. They

17

called out the names of the students in their home-rooms. When your name was called you stood up and followed that teacher out of the auditorium.

I was in the second group with Mrs. Page. So was Chubby. "Your shoe's untied," she whispered as we filed out.

I ignored her. I sure wasn't going to stop and tie my shoelace and risk getting lost again.

Mrs. Page handed out our class schedules. She explained that the seventh graders were divided into flights — either red, white, or blue. We were Blue Flight Two, and we would have most of our classes together.

I looked around the room. There were only a few kids from Meadowbrook. I didn't know any of them very well. My heart sank to the bottom of my stomach. Where were my pals?

Other kids were looking around just like I was. I sighed. We'd been tossed together like a salad in a big bowl called middle school. I think we all felt lost.

When the bell rang we ran for our lockers, the restroom, and our first class. In middle school you change classes every fifty minutes, with ten minutes in between. Believe me, ten minutes isn't very long when everyone else has the same idea.

My classes aren't too bad. I have math, English, and science before lunch, and physical education, social studies, and band after.

The biggest difference is having six teachers to figure out instead of one. The first few days in any grade are spent figuring out your teacher. Ask any kid.

I only saw Becca once. She was going in to lunch as I came out. I dragged her into the restroom beside the cafeteria for a short catch-up. (That's when I found out about the awful rinse.)

Unfortunately, the eighth and ninth grade girls have staked a claim on this restroom. They let us know we weren't welcome. We didn't care. We got into a corner and compared notes.

"I don't think I'm going to like it," Becca wailed. "I don't know anyone."

"Me either. What flight are you in?"

"Blue One."

"I'm in Blue Two — with Myrtle Jones, Connie Haye, and Ella Bywater."

"Ugh!"

"Yeah. What happened to all of our crowd?"

"How should I know?" Becca snapped. "You're the first friend I've seen all day."

"Don't get huffy, Becca. Maybe it will get better."

"Have you had P.E. yet?"

"That's my next class."

Becca had a funny look in her eyes. "Just wait till after you do! Then tell me things will get better," she said.

That's when I noticed her damp hair and flushed

face. I guess I'd been so glad to see her that I hadn't paid much attention.

"You kiddies had better run along before the pablum runs out," a snooty girl said, pushing past us.

"We'd better go," Becca said.

Before I could ask any more she was gone, swallowed by the long cafeteria line.

I had to run to the gym.

That's another difference. In middle school you don't have recess. You have physical education. Boys in one class. Girls in another. I had a feeling it wasn't going to be nearly as much fun.

My feeling was right. About fifty girls huddled together in the locker room while the teacher, Miss Fitz, gave us our instructions.

"Everyone wears one of these gym suits. Everyone takes a shower — EVERY DAY. No excuses. You will have three excused cuts every six weeks. Gym clothes go home every week for a washing. Five points are taken off your grade for a dirty suit, failure to shower, or more than three cuts. Now, line up and get your suits, towels, and lockers."

She sounded like a drill sergeant or a prison matron. You could tell that having fun was very low on her list.

For the first time I blessed Mom for making me wear my new underwear.

We lined up in a ragged line. Miss Fitz seemed not to notice — or care — about our misery as she loudly asked our size and handed us the dumb-looking one-piece gym suits, a towel, and a locker basket.

I heard a distinct snuffle behind me. Margo Wagner, the chubby girl, had tears in her eyes. In fact, they were spilling down her cheeks.

She brushed the tears away with the back of her hand. "They won't have a size big enough to fit me," she said woefully.

"And they won't have one small enough for me."

When I got up to the table Miss Fitz barked, "Size?"

"Midget," I replied, just as loud.

It broke everyone up. Even Miss Fitz's suntanned face cracked in a smile.

"We aim to please," she said. "Would a short-small do?"

"I can always cut it off, I guess."

I held the suit up to me and, sure enough, it came almost to my knees.

While everyone was laughing at me, Margo got her extra-large suit with no one noticing.

"Thanks," she whispered as we all tried to get out of our clothes and into our suits with no one seeing anything.

We shouldn't have tried so hard to be modest. After we ran sprint races on the outdoor track, Miss Fitz ran us back and made us strip and go through the showers. She stood right there and watched our every move.

Nobody has watched me bathe since I was four! With my clothes damp and half buttoned, I dashed for the door as soon as I could. A tall black girl was right behind me. She was lucky. Her red face didn't show.

"That scene was the ab-so-lute pits!" she said, striding down the hall beside me.

"Yeah, I didn't see anything I haven't seen before, but it sure was embarrassing having Miss Fitz watch us."

Our lockers were side by side. We tried our combinations. Neither locker opened.

"This has not been my day!" she said, glaring at the stubborn door.

"Oh, I wouldn't say that. You sure can run, uh — "

"Andrea. Andrea Gibson. And I could say the same for you. You almost beat me in that sprint."

"Cindy Cunningham. And the only reason I came close was Miss Fitz yelling 'Move it — move it!' right in my ear."

Andrea laughed so loud and long that people started looking at her like she was having a fit or something. She didn't seem to care.

"You sound just like her!" she said. "You've got a good ear as well as good legs."

I gave my dial one final twirl. "I just hope my legs hold out," I muttered, yanking my books out. "I've been running all day."

Naturally, I was late to social studies class, provoking a three-minute lecture from Mrs. Massey.

Band was last period. I'd been looking forward to it all day. At least I knew Mr. Larch, the band director. He'd been to our old school several times. But even that class bombed out.

We were packed in the band room like sardines. Just getting my horn together made me feel like a pretzel.

A red-faced Mr. Larch rapped for our attention. "Welcome to Ruffner, all you new students. Welcome back to the rest of you. As you can see we're rather crowded." (That got a groaning laugh.) "I'm happy to have so many students who are interested in band. Unfortunately, we can't make music under these conditions. So this year we are going to have two bands — a varsity and junior varsity" (stunned silence). "This month we will try out for chairs. Section by section. Everyone will try out. On the bulletin board, you'll find posted which day your instrument will be judged. Temporary section leaders will hand out your music. Meanwhile we'll do the best we can."

A tall, freckle-faced boy with owl glasses passed out the sax music.

"How many saxophones will be in the varsity band?" I asked him.

"Six."

There were ten of us.

I put the music on my stand and looked at it. My mind went blank. It might as well have been written in Zulu or Yiddish. I couldn't read a note! Then I looked down at my fingers. On their own, they were moving slowly but surely through the music.

When I looked up, the redhead with the funny glasses was watching me.

Mike McEvern, from Meadowbrook, leaned over and whispered, "Hey, Cindy. Can you read this stuff?"

"My eyes can't," I whispered back, "but my fingers are trying."

"Don't be alarmed," Mr. Larch said. "This is your prepared piece. We'll work on it together. You'll also be handed a piece to sight-read. It will count twenty-five percent of your grade. Now for the bad news. We only have uniforms for the varsity. The J.V. band will wear white shirts, black pants, and a red cummerbund."

My heart sank. The one thing I'd looked forward to was being in the band. A real one. With uniforms and marching. Now even that was slipping away.

We struggled through the piece several times but it sounded more like a cat fight than music. I was happy that band was last period. I couldn't have stood much more.

By the time I got off the bus I was exhausted and depressed.

"I'll call you tonight," Becca said. She looked as tired and upset as I was.

"Make it about seven — I've got to practice," I said, lugging my books and sax up the walk.

"How was school?" Mom asked when I walked into the kitchen.

"At what age can you drop out?" I asked, heading straight for the fridge.

"Mo-ther! Did you pack my white jeans?" Ellen yelled from upstairs.

"No, dear," Mom answered. As usual she rushed off to help Ellen find them. Ellen would lose her head if it weren't attached. Half of my life has been spent finding things Ellen has misplaced. If she had known I was home it would have been me she called. I wonder who'll do that for her in college? I hope she has a very understanding roommate.

I fixed a ham sandwich, got a Coke and some cookies to tide me over till dinner, and went upstairs.

Food always makes me feel better. I slipped into the bathroom while Ellen's back was turned and brushed my teeth. You never blow your horn without doing that. It gets all yucky.

Before I finished, Ellen was pounding on the door. "Hurry up, Cindy. My curlers are ready. I have a dinner date."

"Um brushin muh teef."

"For ten minutes? Come on, Cindy, Kevin will be here in a half hour." Bathrooms are a bone of contention in our house. Three aren't enough.

I came out. "What happened to Rick? I thought he was your steady."

Ellen gave me a superior smile before disappearing. "Nothing happened to Rick. I had a tennis date with him. And he's not my steady!"

25

Boy, this guy-girl stuff is a crock! Oh, I know where babies come from and all that. Mom never tried that cabbage-patch story on me. It's all the hoopla in between that's so silly. Mostly I don't even listen when anyone talks about s-e-x.

After dinner Becca came over and we compared notes.

"A total washout! I hate it," Becca said morosely. "We don't have a single class together."

"I almost got trampled a dozen times today!"

"Do you think our folks would let us go to a private school? Like Northside?"

It was a good idea. Northside is much smaller and parents had a lot more say about where their kids were placed. Unfortunately, in my case, it wasn't possible.

"No go, Becca. Not for me. It costs too much. Dad's already in a bind having two in college at the same time."

"Oh, yeah. I forgot."

Becca doesn't have problems like I do. She's an only child. If I had a nickel for every time I wished I were, I'd be rich.

We sat on my deck and talked until Becca's mom phoned for her to come home. We never came up with a good idea. It was very depressing.

I was so depressed I didn't even write in my journal that night. Evidently the magic middle school wand wasn't working for me.

4

The first week of school you could tell the new students by more than just size. We clumped together in the halls in five distinct groups, greeting each other like long-lost friends. It was so good to see a familiar face that you didn't care if you hated the person last year.

By the second week a strange thing began happening. We stopped looking for old buddies and looked at the people we had classes with all day.

Margo Wagner had been sticking to me like glue since the first day. She was new in town so she didn't have any old friends to look for. She's supersmart and, underneath all that blubber, she's very pretty.

But the prettiest girl in the seventh grade — maybe in the whole school — is Brandy Wine. (No joke, that's her name!) And she knows it, too. It didn't take her long to collect an adoring band of admirers. They all sat together at lunch.

One day Margo and I sat down at their table.

"Ugh! This milk is hot!" Brandy complained. "If there's anything worse than hot milk I don't know what it is."

"I've got some grape diet soda. Would you like some?" Margo asked. She brings her lunch because she's watching her calories.

"Grape diet soda? Ugh! That stuff's only fit for pigs," Brandy scoffed, holding her nose.

"Maybe that's why Margo drinks it," Elicia Morris said with a giggle. The other girls joined in.

Margo's eyes filled with tears. Mine filled with anger. Margo was only being friendly. They had no cause to tease her like that!

A few minutes later Elicia simpered, "Oh, Brandy, you're so lucky. I saw Mr. Zale watching you walk down the hall today. I mean his eyes followed you all the way to class."

Brandy preened. "Really? He was watching me?"

"Well," I said loudly, "that proves the old saying, 'Having good looks doesn't mean you have good taste.' Poor Mr. Zale."

"What does that mean, Cindy Cunningham?" Brandy demanded with a toss of her long auburn hair.

"Think about it," I replied with a grin.

I didn't realize it at the time but I'd made my first enemy at Ruffner.

I knew when I made my second one.

On Tuesday we had a math test. I hate math! I didn't finish my problems until the very last possible moment when Miss Kilper said, "Pass up the papers, please." We did, just as the bell rang.

Wednesday morning Miss Kilper stopped me in the hall. In a voice you could hear four blocks away, she said, "Why didn't you hand in your math test, Cindy?"

"I did."

"Well, I don't have your paper. It wasn't turned in."

Miss Kilper stared at me with her eagle eyes. She's very tall, with a beak nose and sharp black eyes. She's old enough to have taught George Washington.

"I turned it in. Honest, Miss Kilper," I said. I felt like one of the butterflies in my collection — pinned to the wall by her stare.

She let me squirm for a minute before she said, "All right. This time I will believe you. You can take the test in class today while we review."

She made me feel guilty even when I wasn't. "Thank you," I said quietly, but she was already sailing down the hall and didn't hear me.

So I sat in the back of the room and took the dumb test over again. Just as I finished, the fire alarm sounded.

Everyone stood up and marched out just as we were instructed. I stuck my paper on Miss Kilper's desk as my row went out.

29

Unfortunately, I stopped to tie my shoelace in the hall and caused a six-person pileup. It made our class the last to vacate the building. Miss Kilper was not pleased.

When the drill was over I took my regular seat behind Brandy and Elicia in the third row.

"Cindy, where is your test?"

"On your desk, Miss Kilper."

"I don't see it."

"I put it there when we went out," I said huffily.

"Cindy, come up front, please."

With a sinking feeling I complied. I distinctly heard Elicia giggle.

"Show me where you put it."

I pointed to the edge of her desk. "Right there."

"Do you see your paper on my desk anywhere?" Her voice was icy. No wonder everyone called her "Killer" behind her back.

"No, ma'am."

"Cindy, it's obvious that math is not one of your favorite subjects. However, I must insist that you do your assigned work. Sit here at my desk and take this test."

I don't know what happened. Something inside me snapped. "No!" I said, planting my feet and folding my arms.

"What do you mean?" Miss Kilper fixed me again with her stare. "Sit down, Cindy. Take this test!"

"No! I won't. I took it twice. It isn't my fault if you keep losing it."

30

Miss Kilper gripped my shoulder with her long, bony fingers. She flipped me around facing the door.

"Class, do the problems on page thirty-seven. Your homework assignment is on the board. We are going to the principal's office."

She marched me down the hall past the secretary and right into Mr. Zale's office.

Mr. Zale rose and gave us a big smile. "Well, Miss Kilper, what can I do for you?"

She told him.

My heart was beating a hundred miles an hour. Miss Kilper painted a bad picture.

"Cindy, what do you have to say about this?" Mr. Zale asked.

The bell rang for classes to change. It gave me time to take two deep breaths. "I did the test yesterday. I did it again this morning before the fire drill. I don't know what happened to either of them. But I took the test — twice."

Miss Kilper straightened up to her full height. "Mr. Zale, I have taught school for thirty-seven years. I know all of the tricks students play. I have never been defied. This child should be disciplined. And made to take the test just as the other pupils did!"

Mr. Zale looked at me then back to Miss Kilper. "You're right, Miss Kilper. Rudeness is inexcusable and should be disciplined. However, our biggest problem seems to be the missing papers. Cindy says she did them. You never received them. The ques-

tion is, where are they? Did you search very carefully — on your desk, under it, in back of it?"

After a slight hesitation, Miss Kilper said, "I
searched thoroughly for her paper yesterday. I
looked carefully on my desk today."

"Well, let's go see if the test might have blown off
or gotten knocked to the floor or something," Mr.
Zale said in a reasonable voice.

"Fine," Miss Kilper answered.

The three of us marched back down the hall — me
in the middle.

The second-period class was already seated. They
stared as Mr. Zale got down on his hands and knees
and looked all around the desk. Finally, he rum-
maged through the wastebasket on the other side of
the desk. Lo and behold, he came up with my paper!
The second one.

"Here we are!" he said with a grin. "The mystery
is solved, at least one part is."

Miss Kilper's face was crimson. "I never thought
to look in the wastebasket. I'm sorry, Cindy."

I couldn't keep the righteous smile off my face.

Mr. Zale looked at me expectantly. For a moment
I wasn't sure why — then I knew. "That's okay, Miss
Kilper. I'm sorry I was rude." (I wasn't very sorry but
you have to say such things.)

"The matter is closed. You'd better go along to
your class, Cindy. Thank you, Mr. Zale."

"Any time, Miss Kilper. That's what I'm here for,"
he said. "I'll walk you to class, Cindy."

An awed hush fell over my English class when we appeared. I looked at Margo and winked. Mr. Zale spoke briefly to Miss Carpenter and left. The class continued.

I knew I'd made an enemy. Old Killer would never forget. She wasn't used to being wrong.

What bothered me the most was what had happened to my first test. I knew I'd passed it up.

Of course, the news spread like wildfire: Cindy Cunningham was sent to the principal's office. Even Becca had heard about it, although her version wasn't anything like the truth.

"I heard you kicked Old Killer right in the shins!" she said.

"I did no such thing! I just wouldn't take that stupid test for the third time."

"You mean you didn't kick her? Or get expelled?" asked another girl who was with Becca.

"No!"

"This is Helen Bronoski. She's in most of my classes," Becca said quickly.

I really wasn't in the mood to meet new people, but I tried to be patient.

"No, I didn't kick anyone or get tossed out. Mr. Zale was very fair."

I must have explained my actions a hundred times by the end of the day. Instant fame. Of the worst sort.

I was so busy answering questions I almost forgot to check the bulletin board in band.

Garth Stewart, the guy with the owl glasses, nudged me as we left band. "Are you all ready for Friday, Cindy?"

"What's Friday?"

Garth grinned and pointed to the tryout sheet on the board. "Sax section is up Friday."

I went over and checked. Sure enough, there it was in black and white: SAXOPHONE TRYOUTS — FRIDAY, 3:15. Judges, James Calloway, Irene Kilper, Mr. Larch.

All the other words blurred. IRENE KILPER flashed in neon lights. That couldn't be! What was a math teacher doing judging chairs for band?

I ran back to Mr. Larch's office. "This — this Irene Kilper," I stammered. "It's not the math teacher, is it?"

"Sure is," Mr. Larch said cheerfully. "She's an excellent musician. She's helped us out many times."

Kiss varsity band goodbye, Calamity Jane!

I was so shook I almost missed my bus. That would have been awful. I needed to get home before the rumors did.

The reactions from my family didn't help any.

"Is Killer still teaching? She was ancient when I was in junior high," Grace said.

"Middle school," I corrected. "Yes, she's still around."

"I wouldn't want her mad at me," Ellen said, shuddering.

34

"That isn't the point!" Mom interrupted. "Cindy, I can't believe you sassed a teacher!"

"But I didn't sass her! I just wouldn't take that dumb test again. I was right! She was wrong."

Dad cleared his throat. "Sometimes being right isn't what's important."

"Why?" I shouted. "When you're right, you're right! Even if you're little you shouldn't let people walk all over you."

"Cynthia Jane! Don't raise your voice to your father," Mom said, looking as if I'd just spit in church.

"Now, Faye — "

"No, James. Don't take up for her — rude is rude. I think Cynthia should go to her room and think some more about her behavior."

I didn't need to be told twice.

"Please excuse me," I said with extreme politeness. I carefully folded my napkin and walked with great dignity to my room.

There! That ought to show them who had manners. Now they could continue with their usual dinner conversation — boys, college, fashions, college, and boys!

Honestly, sometimes I think I must be adopted. Only I can't figure out why they picked me. Maybe they wonder, too.

I mean, I come home expecting my family to worry about how I'd been falsely accused and all they worry about is my sassing a teacher!

To make matters worse, they were right. Making Miss Kilper angry was going to keep me out of band as sure as God made little green apples. Nothing Becca said could convince me otherwise. Mom wouldn't let me have company, but she let me talk on the phone.

"She's only one judge out of three," Becca said. "I don't think she'd dare cut you if you were good."

"You didn't see her face. She hates me because I made her look foolish in front of Mr. Zale. Besides, she doesn't have to cut me. She'll just give me such a low score that I can't get in varsity band."

"Well, look at the bright side. Band's lots of extra work. We hardly ever get to see each other now. So if you don't get in we'll have more time together."

"Yeah, that's right," I said, trying to sound cheerful.

Grace tapped me on the shoulder. "Could you hurry? I'm expecting a call."

"Certainly," I said politely. (I was still showing my good manners.) I hung up and went to my room to do my homework and practice.

My mind wouldn't stay on either thing. I hate unsolved mysteries! I flopped on my bed and closed my eyes. I replayed Tuesday morning in my head. Miss Kilper passing out the test ... It was a hard one, especially the fifth problem ... I worked the others and came back to it ... I put down an answer and was checking my paper when Miss Kilper said to

36

pass the tests up . . . Jody handed me a sheaf of papers . . . I put mine on top and handed them to Elicia . . . She passed them to Brandy . . . Brandy?

My eyes flew open. Couldn't be. I went over it again. Yes, it was very possible! Possible but not provable. It would have been very easy to slip my test out of the pile and into her notebook!

I was boiling mad. There was no way I could prove it, but I was willing to bet that Brandy Wine had done that very thing. I paced around the room trying to figure out what to do. I never came up with anything.

Before I went to bed I pulled out my journal. Right below "Rule No. 1: Don't laugh at funerals," I wrote:

RULE NO. 2: *Choose your enemies carefully. They might be more important than your friends.*

5

Our driveway looked as if we were moving or having a yard sale.

I saw Dad cramming boxes into our station wagon. I was surprised to see him home so early until I remembered Grace and Ellen were leaving in the morning.

I dragged up the drive. School had been rough. I felt like everyone was watching or avoiding me.

"You're getting paranoid," Becca said.

"It feels more like typhoid," I shot back.

Dad looked as if he could use a break. The station wagon was packed to the roof. Several boxes, two suitcases, and a big yellow stuffed lion were still scattered around the yard.

"Hi, Dad."

"Hello, Cindy. How was school?" Dad asked, looking at the boxes and back to the wagon.

"Awful!"

Dad ran a dirty hand through his hair. "Yes, it is, isn't it? There's no way this stuff is going to fit in here."

I sighed. When Dad has one problem on his mind there's no use talking to him about another subject. Maybe after Ellen and Grace left I'd stand a chance.

"Why don't you rent a U-Haul?" I asked.

Dad looked startled. "Now, why didn't I think of that? Help me unload this mess and I'll run down and get one."

For a man who's so smart, sometimes Dad isn't very practical. I set my books and my sax down out of the way, and in fifteen minutes we had everything scattered on the lawn again.

"Where is everybody?" I asked.

"Your mother and sisters had some last-minute shopping to do. How they can need anything else, I don't know."

"Don't worry. As long as there's a store open, they'll think of something."

"Oh, I'm not worried about that," Dad said. "I'm worried about paying for it."

I dropped the box of linens I was holding on my toe. "Youch! Are we really in trouble, Dad?" I asked, hopping around holding my bruised foot.

Dad's face crinkled in a reassuring smile. "Of course not, kitten! Just don't you grow up on me so fast."

"I won't. In fact, I doubt if I'll go to college. I probably won't make it through middle school."

"Sure you will, Cindy. Don't let one little misunderstanding discourage you. Now, I'd better hustle or your sisters will skin me when they get back. Keep an eye on this mess for me, okay?"

"Sure, Dad."

He jumped in the car and drove off, whistling.

I sat on Grace's footlocker and waited for his return. It was going to be a lot different around here after tomorrow. No more fighting over the bathroom or the telephone. No one to yell at me to stop playing my scales over and over. No more noisy parties, curlers in the bathroom, or lovesick guys hanging around. Why, I'd almost be an only child! Just like Becca. That thought cheered me considerably. I was even nice to Ellen and Grace when they drove up, loaded with more bags and boxes.

My good will didn't last very long. I ran myself ragged answering the phone for Grace or for Ellen. Everybody in town must have called twice.

When Ellen hung up after the umpteenth phone call Grace said, "I do hope you're finished. I'd like to make an important call."

"Are you saying my calls aren't important?" Ellen demanded.

Grace raised one intelligent eyebrow. "Ask me no questions . . ."

"Well, pardon me, Your Importantness! If I'd realized the fate of the free world hung on your phone message I certainly would have cleared the line sooner."

"Calling for the correct time is more important than the conversations you have," Grace shot back.

"Decent people don't listen to private conversations. But then no one ever — "

"Now, girls. Let's not fight on our last night together," Mom said.

Personally, I thought it was just getting interesting. Grace and Ellen don't fight with fists, they fight with words. You can learn lots of interesting things that way.

Dad came in, all sweaty and proud as a peacock. "The U-Haul's all packed and ready to go," he announced.

"Oh, that reminds me, Cindy. You're to go home with Becca tomorrow after school. Dad and I might not be home until late evening," Mom said.

I was stunned. Just like that — I was disposed of. No one asked me what I wanted to do. No one cared about the tryouts or whether I made the varsity band!

"I'm going outside," I said. "It isn't my turn to set the table."

I don't think anyone heard me. They were too busy discussing the best route to take to Creighton College!

I ran out the back door, through the flower garden

41

sprinklers and into the field behind our house. The big sycamore standing all alone in the meadow had always been my retreat when things got rough. I scrambled up to my favorite perch and let out a sigh. Alone at last . . .

A pair of dirty Nikes dangled just above my nose.

"What are you doing here?" Jeff and I asked in unison.

"Ladies first," Jeff said, swinging down beside me.

"I'm no lady."

"Are, too. You jiggle," Jeff said, looking pointedly at my wet T-shirt.

I felt my face burn. "I do not!"

Jeff's blue eyes blazed. "Don't knock it, Cindy. At least you're growing up like you're supposed to."

I was too surprised to be angry. Jeff never (well, almost never) loses his temper.

"What do you mean? You're the one who grew this summer."

Jeff's shoulders slumped. "Not the way I was supposed to. I spent all summer in sports camp. Two weeks of soccer, two weeks of basketball, and two weeks of football. And I'm still not any good in any of them!"

A light went on in my head. Jeff's dad is Jack Johnson — football All American. He played one year for the Washington Redskins. He would have been a pro star except he was injured in a game and couldn't play any more. Now he owns Johnson's

Sports Center. He's a sport nut, and he expects his three sons to excel. James, Jeff's older brother, plays everything. Even John, the fourth grader, is a star in Little League. Jeff played in all our neighborhood games but, mostly, he thought them up. He was never a star.

"So, don't play any sports," I said.

"Hah! A lot you know," Jeff replied, swinging down from our limb. "I don't have any choice. Dad knows what's best for me. Just wait until he hears I was cut from the soccer team."

Through the leaves I watched him slump toward his house. Poor Jeff. He looked so miserable. It wasn't fair! Jeff was smart as a whip. Didn't that count for something? Why did he have to be a jock? Mr. Johnson didn't expect Janet to be one. Why must Jeff? Was it just because he was a boy?

Parents are very hard to understand. When you want them to be interested, they aren't. When you don't need their advice, they're in there with both feet! I guess I'll never understand them. Not until I am one. Then I probably won't understand *my* kids. Maybe it was a medical law or something. I'd have to ask Becca about that.

I settled back in my tree. I knew I needed to practice my scales and my prepared piece, but it would be next to impossible until everything settled down. Grace and Ellen were sure to have dates. Once they left I could get down to business.

I hoped my fingers wouldn't be as stiff tomorrow as they felt right now. I wished Miss Kilper would break a leg or come down with bubonic plague or something. Anything to keep her home tomorrow.

I wished I knew how I stood in band. I knew I wasn't better than Garth, but it was hard to judge with the others. You couldn't tell in that crowded room who was playing and who was faking.

Mom came out on the deck and yelled for me. After the third call I figured she meant business and climbed down. As soon as I was inside she hit me with the news.

"We're having a quick meal. Ellen and Grace are having a few friends over for a farewell party. So hurry and wash up."

"B-but I have to practice tonight!"

Mom smiled her most reassuring smile. "Is it that same piece you've been working on for two weeks?"

I nodded.

"Then you don't need any more practice. You have it down perfectly."

"The tryouts are tomorrow," I exploded.

"Cindy, believe me, I know what's best. Relax. Get a good rest and you'll do fine tomorrow."

I couldn't believe my ears. Here was the most important test of my whole life and my mother wants me to sleep! No. That wasn't it. She just thinks a party for Grace and Ellen is more important. Heaven forbid their good times should be interrupted!

Blinking back the stupid tears that stung my eyes, I said calmly, "Gee, it's nice that you are so certain about me. I wish I was. But don't worry, I won't spoil the party with my boring music."

Before she could say anything, I ran upstairs and locked myself in my room. I refused to come out even for dinner.

When the party was in full swing I slipped out and had a quick shower. It made me feel cleaner but not less hungry. My stomach was growling something fierce, but I wasn't going downstairs if I perished from malnutrition!

I pulled my journal out and wrote:

RULE NO. 3: *Beware when parents say they know what's best for you. It's usually what's best for* them!

6

Tearful goodbyes have never been my thing. Ellen and Grace hugged and kissed me as if they were going to the moon instead of two hundred and fifty miles away.

"Be sure to write me," Ellen said with tears in her eyes. "I want to hear all about middle school."

"Just keep on Killer's good side — if she has one," Grace advised. "I know you won't write but call once in a while to let us know how Mom and Dad are surviving without us."

I promised I would. "You all have a good time, study hard, and come back so educated we won't know you."

"You can't get rid of us that easily," Ellen replied. "You keep Ruffner hopping."

"Don't encourage her!" Mom said. "Run along,

Cindy, or you'll miss the bus. Good luck on your try-outs."

"Break a leg!" Grace sang out as I ran down the drive.

"That's for theater, dummy!" I shouted back.

I don't recall much of what happened all day. I did try to pay close attention in math class so as not to irritate Miss Kilper.

Brandy didn't help matters when she turned around and said to Elicia, "How did the babysitting go last night?"

Elicia looked back at me and smiled. "Fine. Just fine. Mr. Larch has the sweetest baby. I just love little Laura."

Brandy frowned. "I hope you had time to practice."

"Oh, sure. Mr. Larch even helped me with my chromatic scale."

I knew they were trying to psych me. But it worked anyway. I couldn't help it. I felt as if I had two strikes against me before I got to bat. The satisfied smile on Brandy's face made me sick to my stomach. It also made me miss roll call.

"Cindy Cunningham . . . Cindy . . . CYNTHIA."

I looked up to see Miss Kilper frowning at me.

"Yes, ma'am?"

"At least pay enough attention to answer roll call, Cindy."

"Sorry, Miss Kilper. Here."

"At least in body," Brandy whispered.

Elicia giggled — on cue.

All my friends tried to encourage me all day long. Margo gave me her lucky fairystone to wear. Becca arranged to stay after school with me. And Andrea gave me a bottle of black shoe polish.

"What's this for?"

Andrea gave me a wicked grin. "I thought maybe you could paint your face and pretend you were black for an hour or so."

I bit. "Why?"

"Lordy, Cindy, don't you know anything? It's a well-known fact that us blacks got rhythm!"

She delivered this with a perfectly straight face. It broke me up. That Andrea is something else.

"That's better," she said. "You can't blow sweet music if you're up-tight."

I clutched the shoe polish to my chest. "Thanks, Andrea, I'll try to remember." It was easier said than done. Time seemed to creep by, each minute taking an hour. The slower time passed the more hyper I became.

Why did I want this so badly? There was always next year. Or, as Mr. Larch had explained, I could join the varsity band in January if I challenged.

My desire was as hard to explain as my choice of the saxophone had been. All I knew was that when I heard the sax played, I knew it was my instrument.

"Why not a flute or a clarinet?" Dad had asked.

48

Mom shook her head. "I don't think this infatuation will last. Not after all the trouble I had getting you to practice the piano."

I couldn't explain it then and I can't now. There's just something about a sax that satisfies me. I want to get better and better. I want to play marches, jazz, and classical music. I want to be in varsity band. Now!

I went into band class thinking, This may be my last time in this room. I opened my horn case. A package fell out. I picked it up and opened it. Inside were notes from Grace, Ellen, and Dad, all wishing me luck on the tryouts. Mother's note was wrapped around a locket with a four-leaf clover in the middle. "We'll be thinking of you all day. Do your best."

I slipped the locket over my head. Boy, was I ever wrong! They did care. I put my horn together with a warm feeling inside. The warm feeling seemed to unglue my stiff fingers.

"Saxophones report back to band room at three-fifteen," Mr. Larch said when the last bell rang.

My jitters came back full force. I returned to my locker to get my books. Several people stopped and wished me luck. I guess it was obvious how much I wanted a chair.

"Are you nervous?" Becca asked.

"Not much. I just went to the bathroom and now I have to go again. If this keeps up I won't have enough water left to wet my reed."

Becca giggled. She was as nervous as I was. "I'll wait in the hall. How long do you think you'll be?"

"Who knows? Keep your fingers crossed."

"I'll cross everything," Becca promised, crossing her arms, legs, and eyes.

"Don't stand in a draft. You might freeze that way," I cautioned.

Cross-eyed and giggling, Becca took her place with the other kids who were waiting for friends.

Brandy, cool, calm, and superior, was there. She gave me a smug look. "I heard one of your favorite teachers is judging. Aren't you lucky?"

Not bothering to answer, I went into the band room. I checked my pads to see if they were dry and soft. I checked my best reed for splits, adjusted it carefully, and began warming up. Nine other saxophonists were doing the same. We sounded like Gram's henhouse when the dog got locked inside.

"As your name is called, come into rehearsal room A. Bring your prepared pieces," Mr. Larch said.

Thank goodness I was called third. I don't think I could have stood watching any more people come out of that room. Mike came out like a zombie and Kelly came out crying.

I dropped my music when I started out. Garth picked it up. "Blow it sweet," he whispered. That boosted my confidence a little.

Mr. Larch tried to put me at ease, too. "Put your music on the stand, Cindy. Relax. Play your prepared piece whenever you're ready. This other gentleman is Jim Calloway. You already know Miss Kilper."

I nodded without looking up. I knew if I saw Miss Kilper's cold stare I'd freeze. I played my prepared piece.

"Play your chromatic scale, please," Miss Kilper requested.

Next, Mr. Calloway asked for C major and C minor scales.

So far so good.

Mr. Larch placed a sheet of music on my stand. "Take your time. Look it over carefully and play this for us, Cindy."

Sweat rolled down into my eyes and made the notes blur. Hastily I wiped my eyes and then my hands. The piece didn't look too difficult. I took a deep breath, let it out to the count of five as I'd been coached, and began.

Halfway through I missed a key change and faltered. I went back and played it correctly, but the damage was done.

"Thank you, Cindy. You did very well," Mr. Larch said. "You may wait outside with the others or, if you'd rather, I'll call you tonight."

"I'll wait," I said hopelessly. I knew I'd blown it. Old Killer had a perfect excuse to eliminate me.

Like everyone else who came out, I said I'd been lousy. Someone had to be lying!

Mr. Larch finally emerged from the rehearsal room. The room got awful quiet.

"All of you did very well. I'm very pleased with this section. I only wish all of you could be in the varsity band. Now, here are the chairs — until January, that is: Garth, first; Gene, second; Janet, third; Kelly, fourth; Billy, fifth; Cindy, sixth. In the junior varsity: Elicia, first; David, second; Mary, third; and Jack, fourth."

He may have said more but I didn't hear him. My ears rang with "Cindy, sixth"! Even with two strikes against me, I'd made it. It felt like Christmas!

Becca knew from my face. She ran up and hugged me. Later she told me that Brandy had shot daggers at me and that Elicia was crying.

I didn't notice anything. I was a real space case, floating on a sea of happiness.

I'd come back to earth by the time we reached the Morgans'. In fact some of the glow wore off when I realized I didn't have any family to share my news.

Oh, I know sixth chair in a middle school band isn't much to flip out over. But it was important to me. Not that the Morgans weren't swell. They were. But they weren't family.

And, yes, I knew I was being unreasonable. Taking your daughter to college is far more important than any band contest. I knew that, but I still felt hurt and just a tiny bit resentful. If I were an only child, situations like this wouldn't exist!

7

RULE NO. *4: Be careful what you wish for — you might get it.*

Being an only child is not all it's cracked up to be! With Ellen and Grace gone Mom devoted all her attention to me.

"Where are you going, Cindy?"

"When will you be back?"

"Don't you think you should do your homework now?"

"Your hair looks like a shaggy dog's. It's time for a haircut."

"Sit down and tell me everything you did at school today."

Sheeze! I felt as if I had a permanent shadow. By Saturday I was worn out.

When I complained to Becca she just laughed. "See, you didn't know how lucky you were. I told you it wasn't so great."

"Any place is better than the middle," Margo said, munching a fistful of popcorn.

"Hah! You aren't the first-born in a large family," Helen said. "Parents experiment on the first child. Then you have to set an example for the other kids."

"Sh-h-h!" someone hissed in the row behind us.

We were at our usual Saturday matinee, except this time there were four of us: Becca's new friend, Helen, and my new friend, Margo.

We hushed. Mainly because the feature came on but also because it was a pointless discussion. There doesn't seem to be any good position to be born in. The alternative isn't so great either. Besides, we can't change anything now.

The worst blow came Sunday after church. I ran upstairs to change clothes before lunch. I came bouncing back in my favorite jeans and T-shirt.

Mom stopped in the middle of the kitchen and stared at me.

"What's wrong?"

Mom looked pointedly at my chest. "You need a bra, Cindy. I know it's fashionable to jiggle around bra-less, but it isn't good for you. You'll sag later."

"No, I won't."

Dad came in and sat down at the table. "You won't what, Cindy?"

I felt my face go all hot and red. If Ellen and

54

Grace had been here Mom would never have paid any attention! I'd been wearing the same T-shirt all summer and she hadn't said one word. Mom looked at Dad and smiled. "Just woman talk, James. Our Cindy is growing up."

"Really? She doesn't look any taller than she did yesterday," Dad said.

"I'm not!" I declared. "Can I take my sandwich outside? It's too nice to stay indoors."

"Certainly," Mom answered. There was a satisfied little smile on her face, as if she knew a secret or something.

I sat on the patio and ate as fast as I could. I could hear them laughing and talking. My ears burned 'cause I knew it was about me.

Holy heck! Even a girl's body wasn't private. It made me wish Miss Minnie's spell had worked. Boys don't have to worry about bras, periods, and junk.

Gee, won't Mom be thrilled when I get my period. I'll bet she'll have that milestone put in the papers: "*Attention!* Our Cindy has started her monthly period. Further progress reports will follow."

Disgusted, I ambled over to Becca's to break the bad news. I knew Mom would drag me down to Millar's at the first opportunity. When she gets that look in her eye you know she means business.

Mrs. Morgan answered the door. "Becca's not here, Cindy. She went over to Helen's for the afternoon."

To hide my surprise I smiled. "Oh, yeah, I forgot.

Well ... uh ... tell her to call me when she gets back."

"I won't have to tell her," Mrs. Morgan said, laughing. "She always does, doesn't she?"

I stretched my smile wider. "Sure."

I felt empty inside as I went down the walk. The truth is, while Becca and I are still friends we seem to be growing apart. We used to know each other's every move. But not any more.

Band is partly responsible. Varsity band takes lots of time — after school and on Saturdays sometimes. I wanted a chair and I got one. It meant I didn't have time for other things like goofing around, dance lessons, or gymnastics. Becca did. She went on without me ... with other people. Of course, so did I. But this Sunday desertion left an empty feeling.

Without much hope, I stopped at Jeff's house and rang the doorbell. I had to ring twice to be heard over the football game on TV.

Mr. Johnson came to the door. "Oh, hi, Cindy," he said, looking over his shoulder. "Block! Block! Give him a hole! What can I do for you, Cindy?"

"Is Jeff home?"

"No. He went over to the school to try out his new basketball. It's an early birthday present."

"Oh. Okay. Thanks."

Mr. Johnson didn't answer. He was halfway back to the den, shouting, "Clip! That was a clip! The ref's blind!"

Sighing, I walked two blocks to my old school. Maybe Jeff would let me play. If the teams were uneven.

Meadowbrook looked so small! It seemed to have shrunk in the few months since I was there. I walked slowly around the building, peering into rooms. There was Mrs. Graves's first grade . . . Mrs. Scott's second . . . Mr. Kirst's fourth. Even the playground suffered shrinkage. And it was empty. At least, no one was playing basketball.

Shading my eyes from the bright sun, I spotted Jeff perched on the bars at the bottom of the playground. Casually I strolled down.

"Hi! Your Dad said you'd be here — practicing basketball," I said, climbing up on the opposite side of the bars.

"Well, I'm not!"

"Yeah, I could tell. That the new basketball?" I asked, pointing with my toe to the ball beneath us.

"Umm . . ."

"Looks like a good one."

"I wanted an Apple," Jeff said. He fell backward and hung by his knees.

"You wanted an apple? What for?"

Jeff swung back up. "A computer, dummy. I wanted my own Apple computer. Dad could have used it, too. For his business."

"Oh."

"Not 'Oh,' " Jeff said mockingly. "NO — capital N,

capital O. Basketball season is coming up. Gotta get a head start on the other kids. With my height, I'm a cinch to be a star."

Jeff had a bad case of the blues. He was so miserable he made my troubles disappear.

"Maybe you'll get your computer at Christmas. Meanwhile, be a star."

"I don't want to be a star! *Dad* wants me to be a star," Jeff said, glaring at me.

"Why don't you just tell him?"

"I've tried. He doesn't listen," Jeff said bitterly. "Besides, he'd never understand."

I sure didn't have any magic formula to get adults to listen. With Gram gone, my track record was zilch. But I knew Jeff liked to explain things so I said, "I don't know anything about computers. Tell me about them."

Jeff didn't need any encouragement. His face brightened as he rambled on about microchips, software, programming, memory, and other stuff I couldn't understand.

"How did you learn so much?" I asked when I could get a word in edgewise.

Jeff laughed for the first time all day.

"At camp. I snuck off one day with another group of kids. They were in an enrichment program or something. Anyway they had classes in computers. I got hooked. I went every day for two weeks and read everything I could get my hands on."

"Weren't you missed in your own group?"

"Nope. Too many kids. I had my roommate answer 'here' for me at roll call."

We looked at each other and burst out laughing. All of a sudden things were like they used to be. We'd pulled that trick before — way back when Jeff, Becca, and I had been at day camp and called ourselves the Three Mosquitoes.

Our laughter didn't last long. Jeff's face clouded over again as the playground began filling up. "It's getting too noisy here. I'd better get home," he said.

"Yeah. Me too."

"They seem awful little, don't they?"

"Yeah. Happy, too. They don't know when they're well off."

"You can say that again," Jeff said, bouncing his new ball as hard as he could off the cement.

All the way home I tried to put a smile back on Jeff's face but I never got more than a grin.

The phone was ringing when I walked into the house.

"I'll get it," I shouted.

"Guess what?" Becca said before I finished 'hello.'

"I can't imagine," I responded coldly.

Becca didn't notice. "Helen and I were at High's for sundaes and guess who drove by?"

"The Queen of England?"

"Oh, don't be silly! Brandy and Mr. Zale! She practically fell out the window waving to us."

It boggled my mind. I knew Brandy had a terrific

crush on Mr. Zale. So did every other girl in school. But Mr. Zale? I forgot I was sore at Becca as we discussed the possibilities.

After only an hour, Mom yelled for me to get off the phone.

"Okay, Mom. Listen, I have to go. I'm sure we'll hear all about it tomorrow."

"Don't you know it! See you at the bus stop!"

"Sure."

In all the excitement I forgot to tell her the bad news about the bra. I started to call her back but I knew Mom would have a hissy-fit.

I jiggled in to dinner. It might be my last meal eaten in freedom.

8

Brandy was waiting at my locker with Elicia and her other groupies in tow.

"Hi! Did you and Helen enjoy your ice cream yesterday?" she asked Becca brightly.

"Yes."

Brandy waited a moment for Becca to comment or something. When she didn't, Brandy said with a pout, "You did see me waving to you, didn't you?"

"Was that you hanging out the window?" Becca asked innocently.

"Of course it was!"

"See, Becca," I said, "I told you Mr. Zale wasn't taking a lunatic back to the asylum. It was only our good friend Brandy."

The titter of laughter was quelled by a fierce look from Brandy.

"Oh, you two are just jealous! You'd give your right arm to go for a Sunday drive with Mr. Zale."

"Are you saying you had a date with Mr. Zale?" I demanded.

Brandy turned cherry red. Red does not look good on her. "Of course not," she sputtered. "He — he just offered me a ride home from the library. That's all."

"Oh, that's all," I said, opening my locker. "I just wanted to get the facts straight. I wouldn't want anyone to start an ugly rumor."

"What do you mean, Cindy Cunningham?" Brandy demanded.

The bell rang for homeroom. "Nothing," I answered, slipping past her. "Absolutely nothing."

So it came as no surprise when I heard that Brandy was giving a party Friday night and that almost everyone was invited — except Margo and me.

Brandy handed out the fancy invitations before school, in homeroom, and at lunch.

"This is only a slumber party for us girls," she said loudly. "For my birthday Daddy's promised me a real party with a live band."

"And boys," Elicia added gleefully.

"Of course, boys! We'd look silly dancing with other girls."

"You'd look silly anyway," I muttered.

Margo gave me a weak smile. "I didn't expect to

be asked. Who wants a fatso around? But I'm surprised she didn't ask you, Cindy. Everybody likes you."

"Not everybody, I guess. But who cares?"

"I do," Margo whispered, so low I almost didn't catch it. "I hope it isn't because of me that you were left out. I mean you being friendly to me and all."

"It's not because of you, Margo. For some reason Brandy Wine disliked me the moment she saw me. Believe me, the feeling is mutual."

During the week, with all the excited chatter about the party going on around me, I thought about what Margo had said. I did have lots of friends. Somehow I knew the names of just about everybody in the seventh grade, plus a few eighth and ninth graders from band. I'm not sure how it happened. Maybe it's because I talk to people — on the bus, in the halls, in band, and in P.E. I don't remember doing that before this year. I guess at Meadowbrook I already knew everyone or something. Anyway, this year I discovered people — lots of different kinds, shapes, colors, and ages. It was neat.

What wasn't so neat was losing your best friend. Becca was invited to the party. At first Becca declared, "I'm not going if you don't."

"Don't be silly," I said. "We can't always go everywhere together." I thought she'd protest again, but she didn't.

"I guess you're right. Besides, I heard Brandy has

an absolutely fabulous house. Almost a mansion. I'm dying to see it. It's only one party."

"Right."

But everything wasn't right. All twelve of the girls who'd been invited came back to school Monday morning wearing little gold circle pins.

Becca told me all about the party and the pins when she came over Saturday night. "Brandy's house is really super, Cindy. Twenty rooms, a swimming pool, tennis courts, and a bowling green. Really fab! They have a cook, a housekeeper, and a gardener. We didn't get to meet Mr. and Mrs. Wine. They were spending a weekend in Bermuda. But it was her mother's idea about the club — the Secret Circle. Mrs. Wine said at her school they had Greek sororities. You know, groups of girls who were like sisters. Brandy thought it would be neat if we could have a club. She bought these twenty-four-carat gold pins for each of us."

"I guess Brandy is your president or whatever."

Becca blushed. "Well, yes. Elicia did nominate her. It seemed fair. It was her idea."

"What does this club do?"

"What do you mean?" Becca asked defensively.

"Well, the Pep Club boosts school spirit. The Latin Club sponsors the language tournaments. The Pen and Ink Club puts out our school paper. What does the Secret Circle do?"

"Nothing, I guess. Sponsors friendship?"

"Friendship, huh?"

"Oh, don't get so huffy just because you aren't a member," Becca exploded. "It's a club just like the ones your mom and mine belong to."

"Can anyone join?"

"Of course not! What would be the point of having a club? Brandy explained it all very well. We have to keep it small and exclusive so it will be an honor to belong."

"I see."

"No, you don't. You're still back in elementary school. We're going out into the grown-up world now. Some people fit in certain groups, that's all."

"How do you know if you fit?"

"Why — uh — by your clothes, your friends, your interests — "

I interrupted. "Sounds preppy and snobbish to me."

"Are you calling me a snob?"

"If the shoe fits . . ."

Becca threw down the magazine she'd been clutching. "Well, ex-cuse me!" She stalked out of my room, slamming the door behind her.

I wanted to run after her, but I didn't. Over the years Becca and I have had lots of fights. We always made up. She'd come to her senses — I knew she would. Becca Morgan isn't a snob.

I hung around the house all day Sunday, but Becca never called. I didn't call her either. After all, she was the one who had flounced out.

Monday morning at the bus stop Becca was wearing her gold circle pin. Her eyes warned me not to say anything about it.

"Hi, Becca."

"Hi."

"That a new sweater? It's pretty."

"Thanks. Mom bought it for me. For once she didn't buy something weird."

"You're lucky. You should see the stuff Mom keeps buying for me. I think she got the habit with Grace and Ellen. Now she can't stop. She's a clothes junkie."

Becca grinned her old familiar grin. The bus came and we got on and sat together as usual. But something had changed and we both knew it.

It was easy to spot the members of the Secret Circle even without their pins. They were the prettiest and best-dressed girls in the grade. And they were all in Blue Flight One or Two. I guess that makes them some of the smartest girls, too. Because, even though the teachers try to hide it with fancy names, everyone knows we are divided into ability groups. White is average. Red is slow. Blue is the smartest. I guess that makes us Blues the best of the best. The cream of the crop.

That depressed me until I thought of Gram. Once, out in the milking barn, she was explaining things to me. "The cream always rises to the top," she said. "That's where we get our coffee cream and whipping cream."

66

"What do you do with the rest?" I asked. "Do you throw it away?"

"Land's sake, no! You skim some of the cream off for special purposes, like I said. But the best milk is made when you mix it all together. Homogenizing, it's called. All the milk is useful though. Just like people."

I hadn't really understood her then. But I did now. It made me feel better.

That night I wrote two new rules in my journal:

RULE NO. 5: *Friends are like the weather — changeable.*
RULE NO. 6: *All people are valuable.*

9

I don't know what's the matter with me . . .

The house is too quiet. The three of us rattle around in it like the last three cookies in the cookie jar. There's always an available bathroom. The phone isn't hot and sweaty when you pick it up. There's no one to fight with.

That isn't even the worst part. Always before I couldn't wait to get home from school. There was never enough daylight left for playing with my friends. Even on rainy or cold days we gathered in someone's house. The younger kids are still playing. Sometimes they ask me to join in. Sometimes I do. But it isn't the same. Jeff, Phil, and Bobby are all in school sports. Becca, Suzy, and Gina are in ballet, Girl Scouts, gymnastics, or taking piano lessons. It's so organized!

Except for my sax lessons and band, I have lots of free time. I don't want to do that other stuff. Mostly, I ride my bike and read. I spend lots of time at the library. (Mrs. Higgins says I'm trying to read their whole collection before I'm sixteen.)

Mom says my moods are growing pains . . . I hope they don't last long. I never know from one day to the next how I'm going to feel or what I'm going to say.

"Cynthia, I'd like a conference with you at three P.M."

I took the conference slip from Miss Kilper's hand with shaking fingers. Brandy and Elicia smirked at me as they hurried past.

I knew why Old Killer wanted to see me. It was the end of the first six weeks. We were reviewing for exams. I was making A's and B's in my other subjects, but I'd be lucky to get a C in math.

I was nervous and edgy all day. Margo had offered to help me review. She's a whiz at math, like everything else.

"I don't think it's going to help," I replied glumly. "Old Killer makes me so nervous. She circles the room like a starving eagle. Every time I look up, her cold, beady eyes are on me! When I see her all the math I've ever learned flies right out of my head. Lord knows what will happen when I'm in a room alone with her. I'll probably go deaf as well as dumb. Reviewing won't help."

"It might help with the exam. Come over to my house after school tomorrow, and we'll study till dinnertime."

"Thanks, Margo. I'll see if I can arrange it," I said without much enthusiasm.

That's another hassle. Going anywhere when you're in middle school is a problem. You're too young to drive and too old to have your parents cart you around. Of course, there is the Metro Line. Buses run on the hour but they never seem to be going where you want them to go or when.

Just thinking about that conference gave me stomach cramps. I couldn't even eat my lunch. Brandy didn't help matters when she said loudly, "Did you hear about the girl in Blue Flight One who couldn't cut it? They're moving her back to White Flight for the next six weeks."

I pretended I didn't hear her, but it made the butterflies in my stomach go absolutely ape. That would be the last straw for my parents. They'd be so ashamed of me. Nothing like this had ever happened to Grace or Ellen!

The day dragged on. I gave my slip to Mr. Larch and at 2:55 he excused me from band. With dragging steps, I went to meet my fate.

Another girl was coming out as I went into Miss Kilper's room. She looked like Sue Ann did today when I hit her in the stomach with a basketball — sort of white and green at the same time.

"Have a seat, Cynthia. I'll be right with you."

I gulped down the sour taste in my mouth and sat down in the chair beside her desk.

Miss Kilper shuffled some papers around and fixed me with her beady eyes. "I'm disappointed in your work, Cynthia. You have been going steadily downhill since the first week of school."

I nodded. She didn't need to remind me.

"You did very well last year with Mrs. Parks. Not outstanding but certainly better than a borderline C."

I nodded again. My mouth was too dry to say anything even if I'd had something to say. Anyway, how could I tell her that she scared the daylights out of me, circling around like she did?

"You are in Blue Flight, the very brightest and best student group. I expected better from you."

Something inside my head snapped. "Do you like milk?" I blurted.

"Why, yes, of course."

"What kind?"

"Homogenized."

"Do you know how it's made?" I asked and went on without pausing for an answer. "If you leave it alone the cream rises to the top. You could skim it off but if you want the best milk you mix the cream and the milk together. The process is called homogenizing."

Miss Kilper stared at me without speaking for a

71

full minute. Maybe I was crazy, but I thought I saw a twinkle in her eye.

"Are you saying you don't believe in elitism, Cindy?"

"I don't know what that means," I confessed. "All I know is that nobody's best in everything. I think you'd get a better product if we were all mixed up — homogenized."

Miss Kilper smiled. I mean, she actually smiled. "You may be right, Cindy. But what does that have to do with your math?"

"I'm good in other subjects, just not in math. It's the same way for other kids."

"You're very good in music, aren't you? You like music."

I blushed. "Yes, I do."

"There's a lot of math in music, you know. However, I don't think the subject is the problem. You're not a mathematical genius, but you are capable of doing much better work than you are doing. I think the problem is with the teacher."

She said it so calmly that it took me by surprise. I didn't mean to, but I nodded.

"We got off on the wrong foot, didn't we? Over that missing paper."

"I did that test the first time," I protested. "I told you I did. I don't lie."

Miss Kilper remained calm. "I believe you, Cindy. I think we were both the victims of a vicious prank.

But that is past — over and done with. Please don't be suspicious of me. I only want to help you do your very best in my class."

"Is that why you walk around the room watching me?"

"I walk around the room to see if people need help. You never ask."

"Oh."

Miss Kilper glanced at her watch. "We only have a minute or so before the bell. If you do well on the six-weeks exam you can pull your grade up to a true C. I believe you can do that. And you can do even better the next six weeks. Will you try?"

"Yes, Miss Kilper."

"Good. Raise your hand whenever you need help, Cindy. That's my job, you know."

I bobbed my head up and down like an idiot and fled to my locker just as the bell rang.

"What happened?" Margo demanded, running up out of breath.

I shook my head from side to side to clear the cobwebs. "I don't know. I think I just gave a lecture on homogenized milk."

Margo looked at me like I'd flipped out.

"I'll explain later. Is the coaching offer still open?"

"You bet!"

I grabbed my books and ran for my bus. Mr. Phillips doesn't wait for stragglers.

I wish I could say that all the reviewing produced

73

miraculous results. It helped, but I still made a 75 on the exam and barely squeaked by with a C for the six weeks.

Mom and Dad went out tonight to a company dinner dance. After a lot of fuss and hand-wringing they decided I was old enough to leave in the house alone for a few hours.

That's another problem for the in-between age group. You're too old for a babysitter and not old enough to stay alone (so parents think).

I mean, what was I going to do in five hours? Throw a wild party? My friends couldn't get over here if I invited them. I don't play with matches, and my chemistry set blew up two years ago. So what's to worry?

After I assured Mom that I wouldn't open the door to strangers, would call the Johnsons if I needed help, and would go to bed at a reasonable hour, they left. I ate my TV dinner, washed my dishes, and watched a stupid show on TV. I called Becca and Margo and talked for a while. They were impressed that I was home alone. I thought of calling Brandy and doing some heavy breathing into the phone, but then I thought she might like it.

Mother called at eight o'clock.

I did my homework and watched a TV program about high school kids. Honestly, if high school is really that silly, I'm not going!

Mother called at ten o'clock.

I told her I was on my way to bed. I'd locked the house and checked it. And no one had tried to break in yet.

The phone rang again at 11:05.

"Hello. I'm fine. The house is fine. Go back to your party," I said crossly.

"I'm happy to hear it," Ellen said, giggling. "What's up, Cindy?"

"Ellen?"

"The one and only. Where are Mom and Dad?"

"Out enjoying themselves. Or they're supposed to be. Mom's been calling every hour. I thought you were Mom."

"Nope. Just the sister you never write to. How are things going?"

Stifling a yawn, I said, "Okay, I guess."

"Mom said you were doing fine — that you haven't rescued any cats lately or gotten bubble gum in your hair. Any more fights with Killer?"

"Unh-uh. She's okay. How are you?"

"Okay. College is great. I had five dates last week. Each with a different guy."

"Sounds like you're learning a lot."

"Oh, I am," Ellen said with a happy laugh. "Only college is very expensive. That's why I called. I'm a little short at the bank. Do you think Dad would give me an advance on next month's allowance?"

"I dunno. Why don't you ask him?" I said sleepily.

75

"You said he wasn't there!"

"Yeah. Right. Call back tomorrow."

Ellen chuckled. "Okay, sleepyhead, I will. Go back to bed. Keep up the good work. I knew middle school would change you. 'Bye now."

I stumbled back to bed and tried to go to sleep. Ellen's last remark kept going through my head. Had middle school changed me? I didn't feel any different. What was so bad about the old Cindy?

I finally dozed off. I dreamed I was in a dress shop, trying on bodies. Fat ones. Tall ones. Slim ones. Small ones. I'd go into the dressing room and put on a body, then I'd run out where Mom, Dad, Ellen, and Grace were sitting. "Is this the one?" Each time they would look me over and shake their heads. I'd run back and try another body. I must have tried out six or seven models. None of them was right. There weren't many left. What was I going to do?

"Cindy! Cindy! Wake up, honey."

A hand shook me gently. My eyes flew open. Mom was smiling down at me.

"Did I get the right one?" I asked.

"Sh-h-h. Go back to sleep. You were crying. Must have been a bad dream. Dad and I are home now."

She looked happy so I went back to sleep. But I remembered that weird dream the next morning. It was kind of scary.

10

Becca has a boyfriend. It's the "in" thing right now. Lance Wadkins is in eighth grade. He's kind of cute, but he doesn't merit all the raving Becca does. Lance walks her to class. Lance eats lunch with her. Lance calls her every night and talks for hours. Lance . . . Lance . . . Lance. That's all I hear — when I get to talk with Becca at all. See, by the time I call Becca she's used up her phone privileges or she has to get off the phone so Lancy-poo can call!

"I'm going to ask Lance to Brandy's birthday party," Becca announced before she hung up last night.

"Yeah, I gathered that," I snapped, and hung up without saying goodbye.

I was ashamed of myself afterward. Jealousy isn't a nice trait. I missed having Becca's undivided attention. I had lots of friends but no best friend any more.

We are studying the French Revolution in social studies. Miss Carpenter, our English teacher, decided to tie in our literature class with our social studies. She's young, pretty, and full of ideas. Her enthusiasm rubs off on the students. Everyone tries harder for Miss Carpenter.

Monday Miss Carpenter read the following paragraph to the class:

> It was the best of times, it was the worst of times, it was the age of wisdom, it was the age of foolishness, it was the epoch of belief, it was the epoch of incredulity, it was the season of Light, it was the season of Darkness, it was the spring of hope, it was the winter of despair, we had everything before us, we had nothing before us, we were all going direct to Heaven, we were all going direct the other way . . .

"Can anyone tell me what the author was talking about?" she asked.

"Sounds like he was talking about middle school," I answered.

When she and the class stopped laughing, Miss Carpenter said, "Cindy, you have the most interesting mind in this class! No, Charles Dickens was not talking about middle school. He was writing about the period of the French Revolution in his novel *A Tale of Two Cities.*"

"I knew that," Brandy piped up. "Charles Dickens also wrote *A Christmas Carol.*" She glared at me, mainly because of what Miss Carpenter had said about my mind.

I didn't care. I was too happy about pleasing Miss Carpenter.

Miss Carpenter nodded absently at Brandy. "We'll have to discuss your interpretation in class one day, Cindy. However, today I want to read some more Dickens to you."

She was a great reader. After class I asked if I could borrow her book. I liked the way the words rolled out, so vivid and alive.

"You certainly may. But, please, have it back to me by Friday morning. If you're not finished with it, you may borrow it again over the weekend."

You can see why she's my favorite teacher. Not once did she say or even hint that the book might be too difficult for a twelve-year-old. She handed it to me with the confidence that I could read it if I wanted to.

I had to read Dickens's beautiful, terrible book with a dictionary by my side. I was only halfway through by Friday, but I brought it back as I'd promised.

Unfortunately, I started talking to some kids in the hall and almost forgot to return it. A few minutes

79

before the bell rang I remembered and dashed up the stairs to Miss Carpenter's room. I ran into the dark room and almost fell over Mr. Zale and Miss Carpenter. They were locked together — kissing!

"I — I am sorry," I mumbled and backed out. "Here is your book."

I threw the book on the nearest desk and ran.

Downstairs, I saw Becca talking to some kids. I grabbed her arm and dragged her into the restroom.

"Come on," I pleaded. "I've really got something important to tell you."

"What? The bell's about to ring."

Luckily, the restroom was empty. "You're not going to believe this," I said. "Guess who I saw kissing just now?"

"Who?"

"Mr. Zale and Miss Carpenter!"

"No! Where?"

"In her room with the lights out."

"Really?"

"Really, truly," I said and told her about it. "Isn't that neat? That'll really put a kink in Brandy's dreams. She thought Mr. Zale was interested in her."

Becca giggled. "I'll bet she won't go to the library every Sunday now."

"Hey! Don't tell anyone else. Okay?"

"Okay. I won't," Becca promised.

The first bell rang and we both ran for our homerooms.

Friday turned out to be a mixed-up day. First we had a fire drill and then an assembly. It screwed up all our classes. As a result I saw Miss Carpenter for about fifteen minutes. I was glad. I hadn't thought of what to say or how to act.

After school I hurried home and packed my overnight bag. Margo had invited me to go to Maryland with her to a family reunion, and Margo's folks were coming by to get me. She wanted me along to see that she didn't weaken and overeat. She's lost ten pounds the hard way. She doesn't want to put it all back on in one big pig-out.

We had a great time. Her grandparents live on a farm with horses and everything. We rode, hiked, and ate (in moderation) while all the relatives talked and ate. From their looks I can see why Margo has a weight problem. They're all big, chunky people who believe in eating. Every time we came into a room someone shoved a plate at us and said, "Here, take a little piece of this to tide you over until mealtime." Believe me, it was hard to refuse the fudge, chocolate cake, and coconut cookies they pushed under your nose at every turn! I got home late Sunday feeling like an exhausted stuffed turkey.

Monday morning I overslept and missed the bus, so Mom had to take me to school.

"No more weekend trips for you, young lady. Not if you're going to be so worn out," Mom said, shifting gears noisily.

Mom doesn't like to go out in the morning before she's all dressed with make-up and everything. This morning she only had time to toss on some old jeans and her plaid shirt.

The tardy bell was ringing when I ran into my homeroom. Mrs. Page frowned at me. "Take your seat, Cindy."

Jody Craun muttered, "Here's Miss Peepers!" as I sat down. I dropped my math book on his foot.

"Youch!"

"What's the matter back there?" Mrs. Page asked.

"Nothing, Mrs. Page. I dropped my math book."

"On purpose," Jody muttered.

Everyone seemed to be looking at me in a funny way. Even Mrs. Page was cross this morning. While she called the roll I tried to see if I had my clothes on wrong or something. I didn't. Maybe it was just Monday morning blues.

"Cindy Cunningham, report to the principal's office," the P.A. system squawked. I sat for a moment, staring at the brown P.A. box. What had I done now?

A nervous titter went around the room.

"Cindy!" Mrs. Page's voice was curt.

"Yes, ma'am. I'm going."

I felt like one of those poor, innocent French women rolling through the streets of Paris to the guillotine. For the life of me, I couldn't remember doing anything wrong lately.

Mr. Zale's secretary peered at me over her wire-frame glasses. "Cindy Cunningham?"

"Yes, ma'am."

"They are expecting you. In the conference room."

I went in the direction the finger pointed. A muffled, angry voice came through the door before I opened it.

". . . shame and disgrace! Our children shouldn't be exposed to such — such — "

"There you are, Cindy," Mr. Zale interrupted as I walked in.

I was too dumbfounded to speak. Around the conference table sat Mr. Zale, Miss Carpenter, a beefy perspiring man, a smartly dressed woman, and my mother!

"Come in, Cindy. Shut the door behind you, please." Mr. Zale did not have on his famous smile. In fact, he looked grim. "You know Miss Carpenter. The other lady is Mrs. Wine. The gentleman is Mr. Squires, our superintendent of schools. And your mother, of course."

I nodded, open-mouthed.

Mr. Squires, still perspiring, cleared his throat. "Ah — hem. Cindy, ah — uh — it has uh — been brought to — uh — our attention — by Mrs. Wine — that you witnessed a rather — uh — unpleasant scene last Friday."

"Unpleasant? I would hardly call it anything so civilized!" Mrs. Wine retorted with a toss of her head. She looked exactly like Brandy when she did that.

I watched them all — Miss Carpenter with her

deathly white face, Mom in her old jeans and no make-up, Mr. Zale unsmiling — and thought they were all crazy.

"What are you talking about?" I blurted.

"Last Friday morning. In my room — " Miss Carpenter began, her face turning rosy red.

Impatiently, Mr. Zale said, "Cindy, did you tell people you saw Miss Carpenter and me — uh — making out on a table in her room?"

"No!"

"She did too! My daughter came home horrified and disgusted," Mrs. Wine declared.

"I did not! I told one person that I saw Mr. Zale and Miss Carpenter kissing — "

"*French* kissing," Mrs. Wine added, as if proving her point.

"They were not!" I exploded. "Mr. Zale was kissing her right on the mouth — not little pecks on both cheeks like the French do."

Miss Carpenter, Mr. Zale, and Mom burst out laughing! Mr. Squires sat a moment and joined in. Only Mrs. Wine sat as stiff as a board.

I looked from one adult to another. Now I was sure they were crazy.

Finally, Miss Carpenter wiped her eyes and said, "I believe you, Cindy."

"So do I," Mr. Zale said. "But I think we'd better get to the bottom of this."

Mom spoke for the first time. "If Cindy says that

all she told about was the kissing, I believe her. Cindy doesn't lie."

Mrs. Wine gave a disbelieving sniff. Mom's back stiffened. She looked every inch a queen, in spite of her old jeans. "When I say my daughter doesn't lie, I mean just that."

"Ladies," Mr. Squires said in a concerned voice, "let's get to the bottom of this matter. It's a very serious one, involving two of our respected teachers in charges of misconduct."

Misconduct? When was it wrong just to kiss someone? Then I remembered. *Making out . . . on a table.* Even I knew that meant more than kissing.

"In the first place, there isn't a table in Miss Carpenter's room," I said loudly. "And second, I never said that they were — uh — doing anything but kissing!"

"Which, as far as I'm concerned, isn't misconduct," Mom said.

"Well, I certainly don't want my daughter exposed to such suggestive behavior," Mrs. Wine snapped.

Mom ignored her. "Who did you tell about this kiss?"

I looked pleadingly at her. I didn't want to get Becca in trouble. Mom's eyes never wavered. I knew I had to tell.

"Becca," I said softly.

"Where and when did you tell her?"

"In the restroom. Right after it happened."

Mr. Zale whispered something to Mr. Squires and pressed the button on his intercom. "Mrs. Anderson, call Rebecca Morgan in here for me, will you?"

After what seemed an eternity, Becca came in.

Mr. Zale introduced her to everyone. Then he said, "We seem to be having a rumor problem around here. Will you tell us exactly what Cindy told you in the restroom last Friday?"

Becca looked at me. Her face went from white to red. "Cindy said she saw you and Miss Carpenter kissing."

"Is that all she said?" Mr. Squires asked.

Becca hung her head. "No."

"Ah-hah!" exclaimed Mrs. Wine.

"What else did she say?" Mr. Squires asked sternly.

Becca gave me a swift look and blurted, "She said it was neat. And that it would really put a kink in Brandy's plans because she thinks Mr. Zale is sweet on her."

"What?" croaked Mrs. Wine.

"And I said that Brandy wouldn't be going to the library every Sunday now," Becca finished with a rush.

"Slander! They're trying to put my daughter in the wrong!" Mrs. Wine was on her feet, glaring at Mr. Zale and Mr. Squires.

"Calm yourself, Mrs. Wine," Mr. Zale said. "It's

true that I've given Brandy a lift a few times when you've forgotten to pick her up."

"I've never forgotten Brandy! How dare you say so?"

"I'm sorry, Mrs. Wine. That's what she told me," Mr. Zale said evenly.

"I think we've gotten off the track," Mr. Squires put in quickly. "Rebecca, did you tell anyone else what Cindy told you?"

"No, sir. I promised I wouldn't and I didn't."

"Someone must have been in one of the stalls," Mom said, echoing my thoughts. She turned to Mrs. Wine. "Now . . . who told Brandy this tale?"

"Brandy couldn't remember," Mrs. Wine replied huffily. "She said everyone was talking about it."

"Well, I don't see what we can do about a rumor. Tracking it down would only stir up more dust," Mr. Squires said. "Especially under the circumstances — "

"What circumstances?" Mrs. Wine demanded.

Miss Carpenter held out her left hand. A diamond sparkled on her ring finger. "Mr. Zale and I are engaged. We plan to get married this summer."

"I don't see that that's any excuse — " began Mrs. Wine.

Mom overrode her. "Congratulations. I hope this doesn't mean you'll be leaving our school system."

Mr. Zale took Miss Carpenter's hand in his. "Oh, no. I think we'll both be around."

"I can see that any further discussion is useless!" Mrs. Wine said, and she marched right out of the office.

No one tried to stop her.

"I'm sorry. I didn't mean to cause any trouble," I said.

"I'm sure you didn't, Cindy," Miss Carpenter said. "It was wrong to discuss other people's personal lives, but I know you didn't say anything nasty or mean."

"I'm afraid Cindy often acts and speaks before she thinks," Mom said apologetically. "But I've never known either her or Becca to be vicious or nasty. And this rumor was both."

"I agree," Mr. Squires said, mopping his face with a handkerchief.

Mr. Zale looked sheepish, like a little kid caught with his hand in the cookie jar. "It's my fault. You see, I'd just received my mother's engagement ring in the morning mail. It's our tradition to pass the ring down to the wife of the eldest son. I couldn't wait for Mary Lou to have it. I should have behaved with more decorum on school property. That was a lapse of judgment on my part."

Mom smiled at them. "Everyone has a lapse now and then. I don't believe any great harm has been done." She looked straight at the superintendent.

Mr. Squires's red face got redder. "No. No, of course not. I hated to investigate such a silly charge. Mrs. Wine can be very — uh — persuasive."

"Of course you had to," Mr. Zale said quickly. "I'm happy you acted so promptly. But I think the best action now is no action. Do you understand what I mean, girls? Don't go around playing detective. Don't try to find out who started this. Just let it die out of its own accord."

I felt my mulish look slide over my face. I wanted to get even.

Mom recognized my look. "Cindy, Mr. Zale is right. If you want to undo the harm you've caused, drop the matter right here."

"Promise, girls?" Miss Carpenter said.

"Okay, I promise," I said.

"Me, too," echoed Becca.

"Thank you. You can go back to class now," Mr. Zale said. "Mrs. Anderson will give you admit slips.

Neither of us said a word until we were out in the hall.

"What was that all about?" Becca demanded.

I told her.

"One thing for sure, I'll never tell a secret in a restroom again," I vowed.

"Not unless we check the stalls first," Becca said.

I liked that "we." It meant Becca wasn't mad at me for having her called to the office.

We went back to class. It was very uncomfortable. The teacher gave me cold stares and the kids couldn't wait to ask about my visit to the principal's office.

"It wasn't much of anything," I told everyone. "I

89

saw Mr. Zale give Miss Carpenter her engagement ring. That's all."

"Did he kiss her?" Sandra asked, drooling.

"Of course he did! Isn't that what you're supposed to do?"

"So? What's all the fuss about?" Andrea demanded.

"Beats me," I answered. "All I saw was a kiss. Since when is that a crime?"

My answers and the good news of the engagement pretty much shut everyone up. I still had to face Mom. I knew she'd be waiting for me after school. I dreaded going home.

She was waiting for me in the kitchen, looking more puzzled than angry.

"Cindy, why on earth did you tell Becca about what you stumbled upon?"

I'd been thinking about that myself. "I guess I wanted to get Becca's attention. She's been so busy with her Secret Circle friends and Lance that she hasn't had any time for me. I didn't mean any harm."

Mom sighed. "You didn't, but someone did. What you did was wrong, Cindy."

"Why? I didn't start the rumor. I only told what I saw!"

"I'm not talking about that," Mom said quietly. "We've already discussed that part."

I nodded glumly. "Yeah, I know."

Mom reached across the table and squeezed my

hand. "Any friendship you have to buy with gossip or treats or money isn't worth having. You can't stop the clock, Cindy, or turn it backward. People change. You have to change with them."

I fought back the dumb tears that stung my eyes. "But I don't want things to change. I miss Becca!"

"I know you do, honey. And I think Becca is still your friend. Your circles are just growing wider. That's natural. You wouldn't want to give up band or your new friends. You wouldn't like to go back to elementary school, would you?"

"No . . . no, I guess not."

"Good. Because you can't. The best thing to do is allow yourself and Becca room to grow."

I munched a cookie and thought about it. It made sense. I didn't have much choice anyway. Everyone was changing — even me — whether I liked it or not.

Mom sat there looking pretty and calm, sipping her coffee, while she waited for me to think things through.

"I'm sorry they called you down to school," I said. "I'll bet you never had to go to the principal's office for Ellen or Grace."

Mom laughed and shook her head. "No, I don't believe I ever did. Ellen and Grace seemed to grow up by the book. But you, my dear, are writing your own."

My head jerked back in surprise. How had she known? Then it dawned on me that she was talking about the child care book, not mine. I figured I'd better get out of the kitchen before I blurted out something I didn't want known.

I got up from the table and put my dirty glass into the sink. "Yeah, strange things do seem to happen when I'm around, but I don't go looking for trouble."

"It seems to find you quite frequently, though." Mom didn't seem angry when she said that. It was more like she was resigned to her fate or something.

It made me feel ashamed all over again. Why couldn't I be more like Grace and Ellen and make her proud of me instead of worrying about me? Maybe I really was adopted!

"I'll go change clothes. I'll come back and set the table for you," I said meekly.

Mom gave me a surprised look. She knows how I hate that job.

"That would be nice, Cindy," she said.

The first thing I did when I got upstairs was to check my journal — just to be sure. I felt relieved when I saw it was undisturbed. I didn't want anyone to know about this project until I was ready. I didn't want to hear the usual spiel. "You're too young." "Twelve-year-olds can't write books." "What do you know about growing up?" Or worse yet, "How can a twelve-year-old klutz tell anyone how to survive?"

I picked up my pencil and wrote:

RULE NO. 7: *Don't tell secrets in the rest-room.*

That's a good rule that every kid can use. I guess I could have shortened it — Don't tell secrets. Or lengthened it — unless you check the stalls. But I liked it just as it was.

11

For a few days I felt pretty awful, but everything blew over. Miss Carpenter walked around with a smile on her face and that big diamond ring on her finger. She treated me just like she always had.

I tried not to bug Becca with phone calls or demands. It wasn't easy, but it wasn't as hard as I had expected because I was so busy with band. We played for all home football games even though we didn't march and do neat formations.

After a week of silence, Brandy started being friendly!

"Come sit with us," she called to Margo and me one day in the cafeteria. I looked at Margo. She shrugged an I-don't-care-if-you-don't shrug. So we did.

94

"You've lost a lot of weight," Brandy said. "You really look good."

"Thanks," Margo said, blushing.

All during lunch, Brandy was so sweet I wanted to barf. She said, "What do you think, Cindy?" about every topic that came up. The nicer she was the more suspicious I got. What was Brandy up to? It went on like this for two or three days.

One night Becca came over to study for a social studies test. After we finished, she said, "What's wrong with you, Cindy? Why won't you be friends with Brandy?"

"I dunno. Maybe we're natural enemies like the snake and the mongoose." (We'd been reading Kipling short stories.)

"I know you all have had your differences," Becca said smoothly. "Brandy gripes me sometimes, too. But she's not a bad person. She's willing to bury the hatchet."

"Yeah. In my head!"

Becca wasn't amused. "I think this feud is silly! Besides, think of all the other girls who'd be your friends if you made up with Brandy."

"If that's a condition of their friendship, it will never happen!"

"You're pigheaded!" Becca stormed.

"And you are blind as a bat! Brandy's up to something."

Becca left in a huff.

Why couldn't I just be quiet and go along with the crowd? No sense in saying I didn't want to, because I did. I liked a lot of those girls. Why was I so . . . pig-headed?

It didn't help much, but I was right. Brandy was being nice to everyone because of the Queen's Court for Homecoming. Eight girls were nominated to run for the two seventh grade princesses to attend the Homecoming Queen. The queen is always a ninth grader.

Naturally, Brandy was nominated. So were Becca, Andrea, and five other girls. They had two days to campaign for votes.

Brandy bought votes. Not with money. With promises of an invitation to her big birthday dance. "I haven't begun my invitations yet," she would say. "I hope I can count on your support for princess."

I heard her do this routine twenty or thirty times before I said, "Brandy, how many people are you going to have at this party?"

"None of your business!" Brandy snapped. "Why?"

"Oh, no particular reason," I said. "I just thought maybe you'd forgotten to reserve the Civic Center. It will take a place that big for all of these people."

"What people? I haven't asked anyone yet," Brandy lied, flushing.

"Is that so? Well, I know of at least eleven girls who've already asked dates. You'd better tell them they're not invited. *Yet.*"

"Well, I'm certainly going to have more than twenty-four people," Brandy replied and stalked away.

"I hope you're not counting on an invitation," Andrea said, her eyes twinkling. "You have about as much chance of getting one as I do of being elected queen."

"You can't be queen. You're only in seventh!" I protested.

"That's what I mean!"

Brandy and Andrea were elected. For my money, Andrea looked twice as royal as Brandy did.

I did go to the game though. The band played "Pomp and Circumstance" as the queen and her court marched in.

Garth bought me a hot dog and Coke at half time.

Of course I didn't get invited to Brandy's big bash either. I didn't expect to. Only twenty-five girls were invited. That left a whole bunch who wasted their votes, in my opinion.

Becca told me all about the party. They had a live band and gobs and gobs of food. Three boys were pushed into the swimming pool and one girl ate so much she got sick. Becca took Lance and said he was a good dancer, but he embarrassed her when he got in a food fight with some guys.

I guess I'm not ready for the big time yet.

Dad built our first fire of the season tonight. We were sitting all warm and cozy in the den, munching popcorn and watching TV, when the phone rang.

"I'll get it," Mom said when Dad and I didn't move.

She came back as white as a ghost.

"What's wrong?" I asked, thinking for sure that Grace or Ellen had been in an accident.

"Grace and Ellen aren't coming home for Thanksgiving."

"Why not?"

"Grace has some work to do on her independent studies project. She needs to stay and use the college library. Ellen has an invitation from her roommate to spend the holidays in New York. They have tickets to several Broadway shows. Naturally, Ellen feels she shouldn't pass up this opportunity."

Mom's voice sounded hurt in spite of the bright smile she had pasted on her face. I was upset too. There was something special I wanted to ask Ellen about. I'd counted on her coming home.

Dad looked at our sad faces. "Now, now! Don't puddle up on me, you two. It's only three weeks till their Christmas vacation, isn't it?"

Mom gave him a withering look. "You have no sense of tradition, James! This is the first time we haven't all been together on Thanksgiving. It won't be the same."

We celebrated Thanksgiving anyway. But Mom was right. It wasn't the same. I ate three times as much as I usually do, just to make her happy. Dad did his share. But Mom just picked at her food and talked about Christmas.

Personally, I wished she'd stop. The last thing I wanted to think about right now was Christmas candy, cookies, turkey, and pies! There was another reason I didn't want to think about Christmas. I was broke — or nearly so. If you didn't count my silver dollars (which I don't), I had all of two dollars and twelve cents. Even if I saved every penny of my allowance for the next three weeks, I wouldn't have enough to buy the eight Christmas presents I wanted to buy. It was very depressing.

Everyone I talked to at school had the same problem — MONEY. Except Jeff. He has a paper route.

There aren't many ways for a twelve-year-old to earn money. We're too young to work at McDonald's or any of those places. We're too old to take money from our folks and then buy them presents with it. There are no lawns to mow, leaves to rake, or gardens to weed in December. Kool-Aid stands and car washes are out for the same reason. Middle school kids are caught in a bind unless they've been smart enough to save some money all year. Most of us haven't.

I was getting desperate. I was about to ask Mom for a list of odd jobs to do around the house one Saturday morning when the phone rang. Mom answered it. She talked while I doodled on the table impatiently.

Mom put down the phone and said, "Cindy! Cindy, it's Mrs. Horvath. Her regular babysitter has the flu. She wants to know if you'll sit with Hubie and Amanda while she goes Christmas shopping."

"Sure!"

Mom looked doubtful. "You haven't done any babysitting before. Are you sure?"

"Sure I'm sure. What time?"

"From one until five this afternoon. Amanda naps from two till four. She's almost two years old."

"How old is Hubie?"

"Four or five, I think," Mom said, looking more and more worried.

"Piece of cake. I'll take some of my old games and books. We'll be fine."

Mom went back to tell Mrs. Horvath. I was on cloud nine. Babysitting had never occurred to me. It sounded like an easy way to make some money.

"I'll be home all afternoon if you need me," Mom said as I left.

"Go do your Christmas shopping," I answered breezily. "This will go like clockwork."

I was wrong.

First of all, Amanda couldn't tell time. She most certainly did not want to nap at two o'clock — or any other hour.

The words "holy terror" were coined with Hubie in mind. He didn't like any of the books or games I brought.

"Wanna play Star Wars," he announced. "I'm

100

Luke." He picked up the curtain rod which he'd knocked down earlier and hit me on the head with it. "Blam! You're dead. Fall down."

Obligingly, I fell to the floor. Amanda began to cry. I jumped up to tend to her and Hubie began to yowl.

"You're dead! Stay dead."

I tried to explain while I fed Amanda cookies and milk. He quit crying and ran upstairs.

As soon as I could I went after him. I could hear water running.

Hubie was naked, standing on the toilet. The tub was half full of water.

"This is my swimming pool. Watch me dive in!"

"No, Hubie. Please don't!" I made a grab for him but he dodged under my arms and ran out.

"I'm going outside to play," he sang out.

"No, Hubie. Wait till I get you dressed," I pleaded, frantically turning the faucets.

Hubie didn't wait. He flew downstairs and out the front door. I caught him just before he reached the street. I dragged him, kicking and yelling, back inside and dressed him.

Then I undressed Amanda. She'd made "poo-poo" in her training panties. She was very upset.

"You should've put her on the potty," Hubie scolded. "Now 'Manda is a bad, bad girl."

This made Amanda cry harder, which seemed to please Hubie.

It went on this way all afternoon — me yelling NO

101

to Hubie and trying to get the tired, tearful Amanda to sleep.

Finally I picked Amanda up and began rocking her. She was almost asleep when Hubie announced, "I'm going to eat my goldfish."

"Go ahead," I said.

I carried the exhausted Amanda up to her crib. I wished I could crawl in with her.

I made myself go back downstairs. Hubie was playing quietly with his space ships. I began to tidy the house, which looked as if a tornado had blown through it. I washed the dishes, rehung the window curtain, and put away the toys. Just as I heard a car pull into the drive, I saw the empty fish bowl!

Mrs. Horvath came in loaded with packages.

"Mommie!" Hubie screeched and tackled her.

Packages went flying but Mrs. H. didn't seem to care. "Has my little man missed me?" she cooed.

Hubie clung to her legs for an answer.

Mrs. Horvath flopped into a chair — Hubie, packages, and all. "Have they been good?" She didn't wait for my answer, but pulled out her purse and handed me ten dollars. "I certainly appreciate your coming at the last minute. I had to play s-a-n-t-a, you know."

My eyes were glued to the ten-dollar bill. "Uh — you're welcome."

"I don't feel good," Hubie said, climbing into his mother's lap.

"Maybe you can babysit for me again."

I started to decline politely when Hubie threw up all over his mom and the chair, sparing me a reply.

I didn't stay around to see if the goldfish came up. I took my money and beat it. It was the hardest money I'd ever earned.

"How did it go?" Mom asked the minute I walked in.

"Okay."

Mom heaved a sigh. "Good. I was afraid you'd have some trouble. Hubie is well known on his block as the neighborhood brat."

"Thanks for telling me."

Mom eyed me suspiciously. "I didn't want to prejudice you against Hubie. Besides, I thought you could handle him."

Now what did she mean by that? I was too wiped out to figure out her meaning. I waved the ten dollars in the air and said, "I'm going to put this away. Call me when dinner's ready."

Once I got upstairs I flopped on my bed and slept till dinnertime.

Later I wrote:

RULE NO. 8: *Money is very important. There aren't many ways to earn it at our age. Babysit only as a last resort.*

12

Ellen and Grace came home a week before Christmas. I can't believe how anxious I was to see them.

The phone began ringing the minute they walked in the door. The house overflowed with people. I was kept busy answering the phone and the doorbell and finding things for Ellen. I didn't mind it one bit.

Neither did Mom. She was in heaven, smiling and singing as she dashed from one job to another.

It took three days to get Ellen alone so I could ask her my question. I sat on her bed and watched her put on her make-up. "Ellen, can I ask you about something that's been bothering me?"

"Sure."

"How do the French kiss?"

"Just like everyone else, I guess," Ellen said, brushing on more mascara.

I sighed. "No, I don't think so. Because Mrs. Wine acted like a French kiss was something special."

Ellen dropped her mascara and turned to face me. "Explain, please."

I did.

When Ellen stopped laughing like a lunatic, she said, "Mom didn't write us about that part. I keep forgetting how young you are."

"I'm getting a lot older waiting for you."

"Okay. Okay. A French kiss is — uh — well . . . when a guy puts his tongue in your mouth."

"Yuck! Come on, El, don't tease me!"

"That's right, kiddo. Don't let Mom know I told you."

I could see she was disgustingly serious.

"Well, that does it!" I said, marching out of the room. "I'm never — *never* — NEVER — going to let a boy kiss me!"

Christmas day finally came. I got a Polaroid camera from Grace and Ellen. They remembered the photography class I took last summer. Mom and Dad gave me a beautiful, gorgeous pair of Frye boots with boot-leg jeans and a red plaid shirt. I got lots of other small stuff, but those were my biggest gifts.

At eleven o'clock, dressed in my new outfit, I paid my traditional call on Jeff. Just because I didn't see much of him any more wasn't any reason to break our tradition, the way I figured it.

After I'd Merry Christmased all the Johnsons I went up to Jeff's room where Mrs. J. said he was resting.

"Merry Christmas," I said when Jeff yelled "Come in."

"Merry Christmas," Jeff said back.

I thought he'd be tinkering with a new computer but instead he was sitting on his bed with parts of a radio spread all around.

"I hope that's not your Christmas present."

"No. Just an old radio. My present's downstairs. Dad bought us some weights and exercise machines. We have a complete gym in our basement."

His voice was so even — not happy or sad — that I couldn't tell exactly how he felt about his present.

I held out his gift from me. "Merry Christmas, Jeff."

"Thanks, Cindy," Jeff said as he ambled over to his dresser. "I got you something too. Only this year I wasn't too sure what you'd like."

I grinned. "Guess the days of jacks and comic books are gone, huh?"

Jeff didn't answer. The look of pleasure and surprise on his face as he opened my gift was neat.

"Hey, Cindy, this is super! I've been wanting this computer book for ages. I never could find it."

Pleased, I said, "The Book Nook had just gotten them in the day I was there."

Watching Jeff flip through the pages, I almost forgot to open my present. The sweet scent coming from the package reminded me. I tore open the paper and the aroma of summer honeysuckle filled the room.

"Um-m . . . bath powder! It smells so good. Thanks, Jeff."

Jeff smiled sheepishly. "I dropped the box when I was wrapping it. I don't think I spilled any. I remembered how much you like honeysuckle."

"And this doesn't have a bee in it!"

Jeff started laughing. "I'll never forget your face. Your nose swelled up three times as big as normal."

"And your granddad wanted to spit tobacco juice on it!"

We had been visiting his granddad's fishing lodge at Laurel Falls. We were just little kids and couldn't sit still to fish for very long. We'd gone exploring. That's when I got into the honeysuckle with a bumblebee.

By the time I left, Jeff's spirits had improved. He even let me take a trick photo of him lifting a thousand-pound weight.

Becca came over after lunch. She liked the gold post earrings I gave her. (She'd had her ears pierced before Christmas.) And I liked the box of expensive reeds and book of jazz music for my saxophone she gave me.

It was almost like old times as we sat and giggled the afternoon away.

Dad announced at breakfast the next morning that we were going to take our usual trip to Belle Meade.

"Why? Gram's not there," I protested.

"Christmas is a time for families," Dad replied. "Gram's gone, but your Aunt Thelma, Uncle Seth, Aunt Eugenia, Uncle Roth, all your cousins, and your Great Uncle Charles are gathered at Belle Meade. We are going too. Besides, Thelma wants us to see what she and Seth have done to the home place."

"I can hardly wait," I muttered under my breath. Aunt Thelma was not my favorite aunt. And I didn't want Belle Meade changed — ever.

Ellen and Grace protested too, but Dad held firm. We were going and that was that!

The only reason I didn't protest louder was my great uncle, Charles Tallman. Uncle Charles was Gram's older brother. He was the oddball in her family. When he was sixty-five he retired from his chair in the anthropology department at the university and went to work for *National Geographic*. He's been with them for over twenty years. Gram showed me articles and pictures by him lots of times. I'd only seen him once, when I was four or five, so I didn't remember him. But he sure sounded interesting. I'll bet he hated missing Gram's funeral. He was her favorite brother. He was on a dig in Egypt when she died, and couldn't get back in time.

The minute we walked in the door at Belle Meade the tall, straight-as-an-arrow man who was standing by the fire exclaimed, "My goodness gracious! There's Tabitha!"

I whirled around, expecting to see Gram's ghost floating by. By the time I turned back, the man was standing in front of me with his calloused hand outstretched.

"I'm your Uncle Charles," he said. "You must be Cindy. Tabby wrote me about you." He bent down and whispered in my ear, "Do you still want to be a boy?"

I shook my head and grinned.

"Good! Because you make a very lovely girl."

I don't think anyone had ever said that to me. Uncle Charles talked to everyone else for a few minutes and then came back to me.

"Do I really look like Gram?" I asked very softly.

"Spitting image. When Tabby was your age you could have passed for twins."

I couldn't believe my ears. "Was she short and plain like me?"

Uncle Charles cocked his head and peered at me. "Tiny and petite, yes. Plain? No, sir. Not by a long shot. Who said you were plain?"

"No one had to say. I have a mirror. Just look at my sisters and my mom. They're pretty."

Uncle Charles dismissed them with a wave of his hand. "Pretty, yes. But you will surpass them. Your bone structure is much better. Believe me, I'm an expert on bones."

I wanted to believe him. Not because I cared so

much about being pretty, but because I wanted to take after Gram. Gram was beautiful outside and in.

"Maybe I am a throwback. To an earlier generation, I mean," I said.

Uncle Charles laughed. "You're a Tallman all right. Your name may be Cunningham but your genes say Tallman, loud and clear."

I savored that thought all day. It was the best Christmas present I'd ever had.

Christmas was not over yet — not for me. My last present came from Gram, through Aunt Thelma.

Just before we left Aunt Thelma said, "Cindy, I have a surprise for you. In her will Mother left you something. I, for one, think you are too young to have it, but James disagrees with me."

Something from Gram? I was too surprised to speak.

Aunt Thelma continued, "She left you the cherry desk."

My eyes filled with tears. "My little desk? In my old room?"

"It is not just a 'little' desk," Aunt Thelma said sternly. "It's an antique. A very valuable one. Made by Duncan Phyfe in 1793 for your great, great grandfather as a present to his wife."

Uncle Charles winked at me. "Had to keep it in the family, you know."

I swallowed the lump in my throat. "I'll take very good care of it, Aunt Thelma. Be sure of that."

"I'll have it crated and sent to you next week," she said with a disbelieving sniff.

I had a lot to think about on the long drive home. Had Gram known I looked like her? Did she have some of the same feelings I had? Was it because of the Tallman genes that she understood me better than anyone else? Had Gram guessed about my writing when I was little and wrote those silly stories and poems for her? Was that why she moved the little desk into my room and finally gave it to me? And Uncle Charles — wonderful Uncle Charles. In one breath he told me two super things — I really did belong in this family and I had good bones . . .

"You're awfully quiet, Cindy," Mom said.

"I was just thinking about Uncle Charles. He's neat!"

"Unusual, to say the least," Dad said with a chuckle. "At an age when most people retire your Uncle Charles started his second career. And he doesn't plan to slow down any time soon. He told me that he was off to China in the spring."

"That's a Tallman for you," Mom said. "They certainly are a hardy, independent breed."

"Handsome, too," Grace said. "No one would believe he's eighty-five and still a bachelor."

Ellen giggled. "He made me wish I were older or he were younger."

"Ellen!" Mom said.

I didn't hear any more. My head was too full of

"hardy" . . . "handsome" . . . "independent" . . . "lovely." Yes, Uncle Charles had actually said I was lovely. I had good bones.

I felt my face. They felt like ordinary bones to me. In the dark I tried to sneak a peek at Grace's and Ellen's faces. I wanted to see if their bones were different from mine. I couldn't see much but I was going to look at them very carefully in the morning. Sighing, I leaned on Ellen's shoulder and tried to sleep.

I think this was my best Christmas ever.

13

Garth blocked my way into band room. "Cindy, I think you ought to challenge Billy for fifth chair."

"Why?"

Garth's freckles disappeared in a blush. "Because you're ready to move up. Go tell Mr. Larch."

Well, Garth's our section leader. I guess he knows what's best, I thought. So I went into the band office and told Mr. Larch.

All during band I tried to play and listen to Billy at the same time. I hit more wrong notes than a beginner!

"Are you sure about this?" I mumbled to Garth as we left class.

"Sure I'm sure," he answered.

I wondered if I'd lost my feeble mind. Just because you have good bones and a Duncan Phyfe desk doesn't mean you can play a sax better than someone else!

Tuesday morning Brandy cornered me at my locker. "That was a petty, dirty trick you pulled yesterday," she said.

"What are you talking about?"

"Don't play innocent with us, Cindy Cunningham!" Brandy snapped.

"I don't know what you're talking about. And what's more, I don't care," I said, pushing my way through Brandy's crowd.

"See! She's running away again," Brandy crowed. "Can't stand the competition!"

I stopped and turned to face her. "Okay, Brandy. What's eating you now?"

"You deliberately challenged Billy White so Elicia couldn't get into the varsity band!"

"I did not!"

"Yes, you did. You knew I couldn't challenge you if you already had a challenge," Elicia wailed. "You're mean!"

Ignoring Brandy, I spoke directly to Elicia. "I didn't know that. Garth asked me to challenge up. Besides, you can always challenge whoever holds sixth chair after this is over."

"Not for another month," Elicia said. "You only have to accept one challenge a month. Mr. Larch said so."

That was news to me. I hadn't done it to spite Elicia. "Look," I said, "if I lose you can challenge me the next day. Okay?"

Elicia nodded, looking surprised.

"Remember we have witnesses," Brandy said. "You can't squirm out of your promise now."

"I won't even try," I said and pushed my way through the group.

I was furious. Brandy had a way of making me seem like a nerd. What did she have against me? The rest of the girls were okay, even friendly, when Brandy wasn't around. One thing for sure, I wasn't going to lose the challenge just to please Brandy!

I practiced until my lips were numb and Mom threatened to buy earmuffs. When Friday finally came, the challenge only lasted ten minutes. I was fifth chair.

Somehow I don't think Billy cared very much. He wanted to play soccer and band kept him too busy. I don't think he'll stay in the band program very long.

After the first week of school the midwinter blahs set in. This wasn't any different from elementary school. Christmas was over and spring was a long, long time away. There was nothing much to look forward to. Even the teachers felt it. A snow day was a rare treat. Mostly though it was plod, plod, plod. B-O-R-I-N-G!

Elicia challenged Billy and won. Actually, without Brandy she isn't so bad.

✦   ✦   ✦

Intramural basketball was the only highlight of the long, dull winter. After two weeks of tryouts, Miss Fitz selected the seventh grade team. Andrea and I work well together. I'm fast, I can dribble a ball pretty well, and I'm so short people have to foul me to take the ball away. Andrea can shoot the eyes out of a grasshopper from twenty feet and she's deadly under the basket. She plays center and I'm the point guard. There are no flies on Jenny, Lora, and Sarah either. We have a good squad.

Brandy made some pretty cutting remarks about girl jocks but nobody paid much attention to her. I think the Secret Circle is losing its power.

Our class went wild when we creamed the eighth grade 37–26.

In our game with the ninth grade the score was 18–12, their favor, when Andrea called a time-out. The gym rocked with laughter when she came over, bent down, and tied my shoelaces in two double knots. We lost anyway, 42–37. But I think this was the beginning of our class spirit. It's the first time we all pulled together for anything.

The guys didn't do as well, but we were right there cheering them on.

The best thing about basketball is that I've made some more friends. In fact that's the neatest thing about middle school — all the different people you meet.

At home things are pretty much the same. Mom

doesn't ask quite so many questions, but she still hassles me about my grades.

"I don't understand why you can't do better in math than a C," she said when I showed her my report card. "If you'd spend some of the effort you spend in band and sports, I'm sure your grades would improve."

"What's wrong with a C? It's average."

Dad laughed. "If there's anything you're not, it's average. Would you like me to help you with your math?"

"No thanks. Margo's a good coach. I'm just a poor learner."

"You're not a poor learner in other subjects," Mom pointed out. "If you want to get into a good college you have to keep your grades up."

"College?" I yelped. "Gosh, I'm only in seventh grade!"

Mom gave me an exasperated look. "Cindy, next year the college-bound students will be offered algebra. With your grades, you won't be one of them. That puts you behind."

I could feel my mulish look slide across my face. "I don't care if I'm behind. What's the rush? Besides, I won't need algebra in my career."

"And what career is that?" Mom asked.

"A musical clown!" I snapped at her and walked away.

I wasn't about to tell her I wanted to be a writer. I

already knew the arguments for that: writers should have an education. To get an education you need to get into a college. To get into college you need good grades. Etc. Etc. Etc. . . .

Grace and Ellen didn't help matters when they came home for spring break.

"I have great news," Grace announced. "I'm a candidate for the Frankenheim scholarship!"

"That's wonderful!" Mom said.

"That's my girl," Daddy said, beaming proudly.

"Of course that doesn't mean I'll get it," Grace cautioned. "There are five other candidates."

"It's a great honor just to be nominated," Mom said. "I know you have as good a chance as any of the others."

Grace nodded modestly. "I have a three-point-eight G.P.A. And that's with my independent study."

"What's a G.P.A.?" I asked.

"What you should be concerned with — a grade-point average," Mom replied, giving me a significant look.

"What's the matter, Squirt? Old Killer still giving you a hard time?" Ellen asked.

"No. She's okay. It's just me."

"Well, grades aren't everything," Ellen said, laughing. "I barely have a three-point-oh and I've been chosen the Sweetheart of Sigma Chi!"

Mom's face lit up like a sunrise. "Oh, Ellen, that's

marvelous! I was Sweetheart my senior year. You are going to love it!"

I was pleased for both of my sisters. Honest! It's just that I'd like to see Mom's and Dad's faces light up for me for something I did. Just once.

That was one reason I wanted the job of seventh grade reporter. The other reason was that lots of good writers started out as reporters. I figured this job would launch my career.

Our school newspaper, *The Tattletale*, decided to have reporters from each class, not just staff writers. The sponsors and the editors would judge the essays we were required to write.

I thought I wrote a pretty good one. Just as I was turning it in to Miss Carpenter, Brandy came up with hers. "My goodness," she exclaimed, raising one plucked eyebrow at me. "I thought typing was required."

I looked at Brandy's neatly typed paper. It made my inked one look messy. "Where did you learn to type?" I asked.

"Oh, I don't. My father's secretary does all of my important papers," Brandy replied.

"Your paper looks fine, Cindy," Miss Carpenter said. "Typing isn't required." She smiled and winked at me when Brandy wasn't looking.

My hopes soared. I could just see Mom's and Dad's faces when they learned their "average" daughter could win things, too. Of course, it wasn't a scholar-

119

ship or a beauty contest, but it was a start. Maybe then I could tell them about my career plans.

I walked around on cloud nine for two days. I was even brave enough to tell my friends how badly I wanted the job. Even Mom noticed the change in me. "I'm certainly glad to see you come out of your slump, Cindy. You look like the cat who swallowed the canary. To what do we owe this welcome change?"

"Just wait and see," I said in my most mysterious voice.

Friday morning Mr. Zale came on the P.A. with his usual announcements. He ran through a half dozen before he said, "Now, for the names of the new *Tattletale* reporters: Michael Thorpe, ninth grade, Ginger Wills, eighth grade, Lisa Considine, seventh grade. Congratulations."

My head spun. My acceptance smile froze on my face. Lisa Considine? Quiet, gray-eyed Lisa, from Becca's room? I didn't believe it.

"Who wanted that piddling job anyway?" Brandy said loudly.

"I did," I whispered to myself.

Margo awkwardly patted my shoulder as we went to class. "There's always next year," she said.

"That may be too late," I said glumly. "My folks will have given up on me by then."

That night I wrote another rule in my journal.

RULE NO. 9: *Nothing is a sure thing. Don't count your honors before they're awarded.*

Luckily, Mom never asked what my mysterious surprise was or why my mood swung back to gloomy again.

14

Miss Carpenter was responsible for breaking up my blue funk.

In English, the last six weeks we studied grammar. This six weeks Miss Carpenter decided to put our knowledge into practice with a creative writing class.

My heart beat louder than a Sousa march when I got back my first story. The paper had a big red A on it, but that wasn't what was important. Up at the top, Miss Carpenter had written: "Cindy, this is an excellent story. You have a real flair for characterization and action."

These two sentences meant more to me than a Nobel Prize would to Dad.

Maybe I could be a writer after all! The A's kept on coming, along with good advice on how to improve.

With band, my writings, and my friends I was having a blast. I began to wonder why I'd ever dreaded middle school.

Even Brandy's latest snub didn't bother me. She was throwing a pool party/picnic on Memorial Day weekend. Practically everyone except me got a fancy invitation. I told myself I didn't care.

Even Margo received one. "But I'm not going," she said.

"Why not? The way Brandy's talking it up, it's going to be the party of the century."

Margo shrugged. "Because I'm not ready to buy a new bathing suit. My old one's too big. I want to lose three more pounds before I buy a new one."

"You have three weeks. You could lose three pounds by then," I said.

"I know," Margo said, fighting back tears.

"Hey, what gives? What's the real reason you're not going?"

"My big-mouth brother!"

"Joel?"

"Yeah, big-eared, big-mouth Joel! He heard me talking to Mom about the party. He butted right in and said Brandy had asked some high school guys. He said they were a pretty wild crowd. Of course Mom said right away that I couldn't go."

"How did Brandy get in with the high school crowd?"

"Beats me," Margo said with a shrug. "She's been dating Kip Meadows. He's in ninth — I guess it's

123

through some of his older friends. Anyway the word's gone out. Joel says these guys plan to crash the party. That means trouble."

"What kind of trouble?" I asked, thinking of Becca.

"Oh, you know," Margo said, rolling her eyes at me.

I really didn't know. I didn't have any big brothers. And to tell the truth, I hadn't gone to any parties lately. Margo's expression led me to fear the worst. "Won't Mr. and Mrs. Wine stop any trouble?"

Margo raised her eyebrows. "That's just it. Brandy is saying they won't even be there. They weren't at the last party, you know."

"Can I tell Becca about this?"

Margo's face paled. "No! I promised Joel I wouldn't tell. He'd kill me. Besides, it would sound like sour grapes because you weren't invited. Especially if nothing happens. And it might not. Guys like to talk big."

I was really torn. I didn't want Becca to get into trouble and I didn't want to sound jealous. I'm not. Honest. I don't think I'm ready for that kind of stuff.

"Promise you won't tell," Margo pleaded.

Reluctantly, I promised. But I couldn't stop worrying. I was still thinking about it at dinner.

"What's the matter with you, Cindy? I've asked you twice to pass the bread," Mom said.

"Can we help?" Dad asked.

"I don't know," I said, pushing my spaghetti around on my plate. "What if you heard a rumor about something that might happen and, if it did, a friend might get into trouble, but you'd promised not to tell anyone anyway?"

Dad put down his fork very deliberately. "Cindy, I'm disappointed in you. I thought you'd learned your lesson about rumors. Your statement was very vague. My advice is to get the facts or to keep your mouth shut. That's how rumors spread. People will keep passing them along."

"Your father is right," Mom chimed in. "Be sure of your facts. Then think twice before breaking your promise."

"That's right. Your promises shouldn't be lightly given, Cindy. Did you know that my father never signed a contract? His word was his bond. That's what he always told us."

"No one will trust you if you go around breaking your promises," Mom said.

Sheeze! I should have known better than to ask. Parents always turn everything into a lecture.

I hung a smile on my face. "Thanks. I guess that settles it. First, I'll check my facts."

"Good girl," Dad said.

"Finish your dinner," Mom said, looking pleased.

I ate a few more bites and excused myself from the table.

I knew they meant well, but they didn't understand. Becca is my friend, even if she has grown up faster than I have. Margo is my friend too. Either way I went I was on a guilt trip.

How could I get facts? I didn't know any high school kids. Even if I did, what could I say? Hey, guys, are you all going to crash Brandy's party and cause trouble? Fat chance!

I was so worried that Margo tried to pump some more information out of Joel. He shut up like a clam.

"He told me to bug off," Margo said. "He even threatened to tell Mom I've been feeding my breakfast to the cat. I can't ask him any more, Cindy."

I understood Margo's position. Occasionally I'd been blackmailed like that by Grace or Ellen. But understanding didn't ease the guilt I felt every time I thought about what might happen to Becca. What awful things did party crashers do, anyway?

Miss Carpenter's announcement drove the party crashers right out of my head.

"Class, I have some very exciting news. The Literary Guild is sponsoring a local creative writing contest for students in Ruffner Middle School. The categories are essay, poetry, and short story. First place winners will receive twenty-five dollars; second place, fifteen; third place, ten. The first place winners will have their work entered in the state creative writing contest, which will be held in August. We have some excellent writers in this class

126

and I urge you to enter. The deadline is May twenty-second — ten days from today."

Miss Carpenter looked straight at me when she said the part about entering. I didn't need any urging. This was better than a reporter's job any day. I planned to enter and win one of those prizes.

"You are going to enter, aren't you, Cindy?" Miss Carpenter asked as we filed out of class.

"Yes, ma'am, I — "

"So am I, Miss Carpenter," Brandy interrupted. "I've already thought of my topic."

"Good. Begin work on it right away. Ten days isn't very long."

Brandy gave me a snooty look and walked away.

Well, I'll show her! I'll write my essay and this time I'll even have it typed. I could hardly wait to get home and go to work.

I was so pumped up that I beat Andrea in the 50-yard dash.

"Are you on something?" Andrea panted. "Speed, maybe?"

"Nope!" I grinned, holding my sides. "Just a natural high."

"Don't tell me! Let me guess. You won a million dollar sweepstakes!"

"Unh-uh. The stakes are much lower than that — moneywise. But better than money, otherwise."

"Bite your tongue, girl! What could be better than a million dollars?"

127

While we loped around the track I told her.

"I like it," Andrea said with a happy grin. "I hope you win but, most of all, I hope you beat that stuck-up Brandy!"

"That did cross my mind," I said with a chuckle.

"You know what she said to me last fall at Homecoming? She said in that lah-de-dah voice of hers, 'I'm so glad you're a princess with me, Andrea. It's good for your people.'"

I stopped in the middle of the track. "And what did you say?"

Andrea gave me a wicked grin. "You don't want to hear, girl. That red on her cheeks wasn't make-up, believe me."

"I guess we're lucky that there aren't more like her around. One Brandy is enough."

"One too many, if you ask me," Andrea said. "Go for it! Take her down a peg or two."

"I'm going to give it my best shot," I vowed.

I did try. Very hard. I mean, I gave up my Saturday matinee and a hike to Maymount Park with Jeff on Sunday. I sat at my desk and wrote, even though it was a beautiful spring weekend. All I had to show for my efforts was a wastebasket full of paper. The ideas were there, but they wouldn't go down on paper.

I wasn't too worried. After all, I had a whole week.

"How are you doing on your entry?" Brandy asked

Monday morning. Sugar dripped from every word.

"Fine," I answered and slammed my locker.

"That's wonderful!" Brandy paused, waiting for me to ask about her entry, I guess. When I didn't say anything she continued, "Mine's going very well. In fact I already have my first draft."

"Oh-h! Aren't you smart," Elicia said. "What's your topic, Brandy?"

"I guess I shouldn't tell my competition," Brandy said, smiling. "But I know Cindy wouldn't steal my idea. I'm entering an essay — 'What America Means to Me.' "

The satisfied grin on her face made me want to puke. It didn't take a genius to figure out her flag-waving strategy. "Sounds great," I said. "I'm sure the judges will love it."

Brandy's eyes shot poisoned darts at me. She's no dummy. She knew I was on to her. Right on cue, Elicia asked her *next* prepared question. "What's your category, Cindy? Short story?"

"No. Essay."

"And what's your topic?" Sandra asked.

"I haven't decided yet," I replied, looking Brandy straight in the eye. "Maybe apple pie or mother-hood."

Sandra and Elicia didn't understand. Brandy did.

"I thought you said you were doing fine," Sandra said scornfully. "You haven't even picked a topic."

"She's just afraid to tell us," Elicia said.

"No," Brandy said, looking me over critically. "It's just that Cindy is unprepared as usual. Too bad you can't wear boots all year round, Cindy."

I looked down. Sure enough, my shoelaces on my brand new shoes were untied. I grinned. Old Brandy was fighting back.

"Why are you standing here grinning?" Margo asked, giving me a shove. "The bell's rung. We'll be late to class."

On the way to class I told her about the prepared skit that had just been put on.

"Don't let her upset you," Margo said. "Just do your thing."

"I'm not upset. I just can't figure her out. Why does she dislike me in particular?"

Margo didn't have time to answer. Mrs. Page was calling roll. I didn't need another tardy mark beside my name so I slipped quietly into my seat.

Later, during our math test, Margo got up to sharpen her pencil and dropped a note on my desk. I unfolded the note. It said: "You-know-who wants to be Miss Everything of Ruffner Middle School. You're standing in her way."

I couldn't help it, I giggled out loud. I had a quick mental picture of Mr. Zale placing a crown on Brandy's head and saying, "I crown you MISS EVERY-THING."

"What's so funny, Cindy?" Miss Kilper asked. She was standing beside my desk.

"N-nothing, Miss Kilper." I covered the note with

my left hand. I held my breath. I knew it looked like Margo and I were cheating.

My maneuver didn't fool Miss Kilper. Very gently she lifted my hand and read the note.

A slight smile lifted the corners of Miss Kilper's mouth. It was gone in a flash. "You're on the right track with this problem," she said solemnly. "Carry on."

I felt lightheaded. Then I realized I was still holding my breath. I let it out with a whoosh. I looked back at Margo. She was stiff with fear. Her face was as white as her note. I made a thumbs-up sign and she slumped back with relief.

I buckled down and finished my test with a few minutes to spare.

Margo's note gave me a quick fix of laughter, but I was more worried than I had admitted. Brandy already had a topic (puky as it was) and a first draft. All I had was a wastebasket full of crumpled paper and a bunch of ideas.

I resolved to go straight home from school and get to work.

Good intentions do not write essays. Garth called a sax section practice after school for Monday and Tuesday. That wouldn't have been so bad if each of my teachers hadn't piled on homework. Why don't they check with each other before they assign everything for one week?

By Thursday I was in a panic.

131

"You must be famished," Mom said. "The way you are shoveling in food, one would think you hadn't eaten in a week."

"Lots of work to do," I answered, gulping down my last piece of pie. "May I be excused?"

Before Mom could answer there was a loud banging at the back door. Mrs. Johnson burst into the room.

"I am sorry. This is an emergency! Cindy, have you seen Jeff?"

I looked at her blankly. "Uh — yeah, I think he was on the bus this morning."

"Are you positive? Did you see him in school?"

"What's the matter, Julie?" Mom asked.

Mrs. Johnson didn't pay any attention to her. She was staring at me imploringly. "Think, Cindy," she begged.

My mind went blank for a moment. Everyone waited. Finally, I could picture Jeff at the bus stop. He was wearing jeans and a red T-shirt. His backpack was slung over his shoulder, his blue gym bag in his right hand. He got on after I did and went to the back of the bus. I don't recall seeing him after that.

I told Mrs. Johnson.

She collapsed on a chair and starting crying. "Jeff's run away," she sobbed.

Dad went to get her some water. Mom put her arms around Mrs. Johnson and patted her. I stood there with my mouth open.

Between sobs, Mrs. Johnson told us the story. "I didn't miss him until dinner. Things are so hectic with all the different schedules. Janet's dance class, baseball practice, Little League, Jack's work. I set his place and he never came to dinner. He didn't have anything scheduled on the calendar. I thought maybe he was sleeping. I went up to his room and found the note. He said he — he was going away and for me not to worry — he'd be fine."

"He will," Dad said. "Jeff's a smart boy."

"He's only twelve. Where will he go? How will he eat?" Mrs. Johnson cried, rocking back and forth.

"Maybe he's staying with a friend," Mom ventured.

"I've called all his friends. No one saw him in school. They thought he was sick."

"Have you called the police?" Dad asked.

"Yes, but they weren't much help. They said he hadn't been gone long enough."

"Why did he leave? Did you have a fight?" I asked.

"Cindy!"

"That's all right, Faye. It's what the police asked, too," Mrs. Johnson said. "No, Cindy, we didn't have a fight. None of us. Jeff's been moody lately but he hasn't fought with anyone. You're one of his best friends. Do you know anything at all about this? Please tell me if you do."

Her words stung like a slap in the face. Some

133

friend I was! I wouldn't even go for a hike with him last Saturday.

"I don't know anything," I protested.

Mrs. Johnson looked defeated. "I thought he might have told you his plans . . ."

I shook my head.

Dad touched my shoulder. "This is serious, Cindy. It isn't one of your games, is it?"

"No! I don't have any idea where Jeff is."

Mrs. Johnson jumped to her feet. "I must get back. Jack's calling the hospitals. The children are searching the neighborhood. I — I don't know what else to do . . ."

"Let us know if we can help in any way," Mom said. "And try not to worry so much. Jeff can take pretty good care of himself."

"I'll drive around the city and see if I can see him," Dad said.

"I'll go with you. I know some of the places Jeff hangs out," I volunteered.

We looked everywhere I could think of — the old playground, the park, the game parlors — but we didn't find one trace of Jeff. The Johnsons had the same results.

Jeff had vanished like a ghost in daylight.

15

Becca was waiting for me at the bus stop. Her face looked as sad as I felt. "Have they heard anything about Jeff yet?"

"Nothing yet. Mr. Johnson is checking out the bus station and stuff this morning."

Becca gulped. "You mean they think he ran away?"

"Yeah. What else? He left a note."

"Oh . . . Well, we didn't know that," Becca said, her face shining with relief. "Mom thought he'd been kidnapped. That happens, you know. Young boys and girls simply are missing. Hundreds each year. Mom almost wouldn't let me ride the school bus."

By now the other kids had gathered around — all ears.

"Why'd he run away, Cindy?" Phil asked.

"How should I know?" I snapped. I whirled around and gave Phil my meanest glare. Why did everyone think I should be in on Jeff's schemes?"

"Sheeze! Don't get mad, Cindy. I thought you'd know. You're close to the Johnsons, aren't you?"

"Well, I don't know any more than you do. And that isn't much. Jeff's supposed to be your friend, too."

The kids all drifted away. All except Becca. She put her hand on my arm and said, "I feel just as bad as you do, Cindy. Jeff's been awful different this year. Maybe we should have paid more attention."

I shook off her hand. "Yeah, that's easy to say now but it doesn't bring Jeff back."

Becca knew me pretty well. She knew I wasn't mad at her so she didn't back away. "Do you know why he ran away?"

"Maybe. Maybe I have an idea. It wasn't anything we could have changed."

"Then you're worried about what will happen to him?"

"For gosh sakes, Becca! Aren't you? He's only twelve. What's he going to do? Join the army? Work on a farm? In a factory?"

"You're forgetting something, Cindy. If Jeff ran away you can bet he had a plan. A good one."

Becca was right. In all the fuss and hoopla, I'd forgotten who it was that ran away. Jeff would have had a good plan. That meant no one was going to find him until he wanted to be found.

I smiled for the first time in hours. "You're right, Becca. Thanks!"

Becca looked puzzled. "For what? It's still pretty serious. Jeff's plans could go haywire."

The bus came and spared me an answer. Becca didn't know Jeff like I did. I had a lot of faith in his ability.

My faith was justified. After listening to the buzz of rumors and speculations all day, I came home to find that, sure enough, Jeff had had a clever, well-thought-out plan.

"He must have been working on this for over a week," Mom said, shaking her head. "He withdrew money from his savings account — told the bank teller he was buying a moped for his paper route. Then he found a boy to take his route, and then he quit. Mr. Franklin wasn't suspicious. Jeff told him he'd be away for the summer."

"Well, he is," I said defensively. Mom's voice was condemning Jeff. She seemed amazed that anyone under thirty could have a plan and carry it out.

Mom ignored me. "That isn't all. Jeff rode the bus to school and went into his homeroom so he wouldn't be missed at first. After that he vanished. No one remembers him at the bus station, hitchhiking, or anywhere. The police are not very encouraging. The Johnsons are frantic."

"Jeff can take care of himself," was all I allowed myself to say. I wanted to say, "Why didn't they show more concern when he was home?" but I didn't. Mom wasn't listening anyway.

"Jeff's mother can't understand why he ran away," she said. "The police keep yammering at her to find a cause for Jeff's leaving, but she doesn't know any."

"Would that bring him back?"

Mom's eyes finally focused on me. "No. You're right. It wouldn't. I wonder why they keep harping on it."

I shrugged. "Who knows? Say, can I take some juice and cookies upstairs? I have some important work to get done."

Instead of being upset, Mom said, "That's fine. I'm taking a casserole over to the Johnsons. I'm sure Julie doesn't feel like cooking. Our dinner will be at six." Usually she never allows food upstairs without a lecture.

I went upstairs, changed my clothes, ate my snack, got out clean paper, sharpened my pencil, and sat down at my desk. I was all prepared for an hour and a half of writing before dinner.

Instead the blank paper glared at me. The blue lines squiggled around and formed Jeff's face. I shut my eyes. When I opened them Jeff was gone. The page was blank again, the lines back in place. I tried to think about my essay but my mind kept running backward . . .

Back to second grade when Jeff and I broke out with chicken pox on the same day. We weren't very sick, but no one could play with us. Finally our folks let us get together. We made a tent out of a sheet from Jeff's bed and played cowboys and Indians all day. When Becca broke out she joined us.

. . . And the summer we built the raft! The one that sank in the middle of the pond with Jeff on board. We saved Jeff but not my brand new scout knife and all our supplies — six peanut butter sandwiches and a bag of potato chips.

. . . Or the Halloween when we decided to find out once and for all if Mr. Zalurski was a Soviet spy! That was Jeff's contention. He was certain the big antenna in the back yard meant a hidden transmitter where Mr. Z. got in contact with Soviet submarines.

Becca and I were to dress in different costumes and ring Mr. Z.'s bell for trick-or-treat while Jeff inspected the back of the house.

I laughed out loud when I thought of what happened.

I wasn't laughing at the time, though, because I broke my arm. After Becca and I had each gone to the door twice, Becca began to get cold feet. I mean she wanted to quit and go trick-or-treating for real. Jeff still hadn't come back. I talked Becca into going up to the door one more time while I tried to find Jeff. She went and I ran. Ran right into the open coal chute and fell kerplunk on top of Jeff! It didn't hurt him, but I landed funny on my arm and spent the rest of that Halloween in the Emergency Room at the hospital, getting a cast put on. Jeff stayed with me. He was the first one to sign my cast. Mr. Zalurski was second. He wasn't even angry with us. The next day he invited us over to watch him broadcast over his ham radio. He let us talk to a man in Nova Scotia!

My eyes filled with tears as I remembered other times . . . The chemistry experiment that went wrong and burned a hole in Mrs. Johnson's mahogany table. The poisonous mushrooms we'd picked and tried to sell to get money for a second trip to the circus. Only Mom's alertness saved us from killing half the neighborhood . . .

I wiped my tears away and pushed my papers aside. Why was I crying? Jeff wasn't dead or anything. In fact, he was probably having a high old time wherever he was.

But still, I couldn't concentrate on writing an essay. Instead I did my homework until Mom called me for dinner.

By Friday, interest in Jeff had simmered down at school, but the interest in my essay hadn't lessened any. Brandy was still on my case.

"How is your essay coming along?" she or one of her friends had asked — *every* day.

"What did you say your topic was?" Sandra asked, all innocent and wide-eyed.

140

"I didn't say. And before you ask, the essay is coming along very well!" I snapped.

"Well, ex-cuse me!" Sandra said huffily.

Margo waited until Sandra had run off to report to Brandy before she said, "You aren't a very good liar, Cindy."

"Oh, yeah?"

"Unh-uh. Your face gets all white and sweaty."

"I'm hot from P.E.!" I protested.

Margo wasn't buying my story. "You haven't even started it, have you?"

"No," I admitted. "The ideas are rolling around in my head but they won't go down on paper."

"Because of Jeff?"

I nodded, miserable. "I want to win that contest in the worst way. But every time I sit down to write all I can think of is Jeff and what a lousy friend I am."

"You're not a lousy friend! Even if you were, how does it help Jeff for you not to enter the contest?"

"Margo's right," Becca said. "Don't let Brandy beat you by default. She's even tried to bribe me to find out your topic. That's sick! You've got to enter, Cindy."

We were huddled around my locker before social studies class. I shut my locker firmly. "I'm going to enter that contest if I have to write 'Mary Had a Little Lamb.' I have all weekend. I'm not coming out of my room till it's done. So don't worry."

"Atta girl!" Margo cheered.

"All *right,* Cindy!" Becca said with a pleased laugh. "You're not a quitter!"

The support of my friends made me feel better. I was smiling when I went in to band.

"That's much better," Garth said while I was getting out my sax.

"What's better?"

"You — I thought you might never smile again," Garth said. Then he blushed and his freckles did their vanishing act. "I — uh — I'm sorry about your — uh — boyfriend."

For a moment I didn't understand. "Jeff? Jeff's not my boyfriend. I mean, he is my friend and he is a boy. But not together. See?"

The funniest look came over Garth's face. He pushed his glasses up on his nose, like he always does, and grinned. "Anyway — whatever, I'm glad you feel better."

"Thanks."

I did feel better. Even when Miss Carpenter stopped by my locker after school and reminded me that the deadline was Monday, I still felt confident. I knew I could write that essay tonight, have it typed tomorrow, and turn it in on time.

I walked into my house full of enthusiasm.

I heard voices in the kitchen. I don't know why, but I walked quietly down the hall and peeked around the corner.

Mom and Mrs. Johnson were sitting in the breakfast nook. Mrs. Johnson held her head in her hands.

"Julie, you're making yourself ill," Mom was saying. "You have to snap out of this."

Mrs. Johnson took her hands away. I hardly recognized the baggy-eyed, deathly pale woman sitting at our table.

"I know. Everything is being done that can be done. But it's so hard, Faye. Especially when I get my hopes up. When someone calls and says they think they've seen Jeff, I'm so happy. Then it turns out to be a false lead and I want to die." Fresh tears flowed down her cheeks.

"Oh, Julie. Please don't cry so. People mean well. They're trying to help," Mom said, passing her some Kleenex from a box at her elbow.

"But where is he? If I only knew he was safe!"

"I'm sure he is. Honest, Julie. I just feel it deep in my bones."

Mrs. Johnson mopped her face. "Feelings! I don't trust feelings any more, Faye. I *felt* everything was fine at home. We had a wonderful, happy family. Or so I thought. We were doing everything possible for our children. You know how Jack and I have always wanted to go to Hawaii? Well, this was going to be the year. *Was.* But Jack pulled some strings and was able to get James and Jeff in the best sports camp in the country — Englebrook. It's very expensive. I didn't mind one bit. Our boys are worth it. Jack told the boys two weeks ago. They were so happy . . ."

I didn't stick around to hear any more. Now I

knew why Jeff had run away. He couldn't stand another summer in a sports camp.

Why hadn't he just told them? Why did he feel he had to run away? Did he know what this was doing to his mom? No way! Jeff loved his parents, especially his mom. So where on earth was he?

I slipped upstairs and sat for a long time looking out the window at Jeff's house, at the big oak where we'd built a tree house, at the jungle gym where we'd played every summer . . . Finally, I saw Mrs. Johnson's slumped figure going home.

With a sigh I went over to my desk. Moping about Jeff wasn't going to get my paper written. I pulled out a fresh sheet of paper and wrote: "Survival Manual for Your First Year of Middle School."

The blank spaces looked enormous below the title. What did I know about survival?

Nothing.

I looked hopelessly around my room. Where was Jeff? The box of honeysuckle bath powder sitting on my dresser reminded me of happier times. It was almost empty . . .

A rocket went off in my head. That's where Jeff was! It had to be Laurel Falls. No — wait a minute. His grandparents sold the cabin when they moved to Florida two years ago. That's why we hadn't been back.

The floral box drew me like a magnet. I picked it up and smelled the summery smell.

144

It was crazy but I knew as well as I knew my own name — Cynthia Jane Cunningham — that Jeff was at Laurel Falls.

I was so excited that I started to run over and tell Mrs. Johnson. My hand was on the doorknob when I remembered what she had said about false hopes. What if I was wrong?

I also remembered Dad's stern warning about checking your facts. So far I'd listened to him. I hadn't found any facts about the party-crashers so I hadn't told Becca one single word. But this was different, wasn't it?

When Mom called me to dinner I was still wrestling with the problem. I ate quickly and excused myself before Mom could start asking questions. She has a way of sensing when I'm hiding something.

By the time I reached my room I'd decided I would slip off and see for myself. That way no one would be hurt if I was wrong. I was pretty certain — but just in case . . .

I chewed the eraser off my best pencil before I came up with a workable plan.

I slipped downstairs into Dad's study and found the road atlas. It took me a few minutes, but I found Laurel Forks. It didn't seem too far — just an inch or so.

Laurel Forks is a little town — really two stores and a gas station — that is just before the turnoff to Laurel Falls. Once, Jeff and I had hiked down to the store for ice cream. If I could get to Laurel Forks I could walk up to the cabin.

I tiptoed back upstairs to the hall phone. My heart was pounding in a very funny way when I dialed the bus terminal.

"Trailways. May I help you?"

"Yes. What time can I get a bus to Laurel Forks in the morning?" I hoped my voice sounded very grown up.

"Laurel Forks? Just a minute, please."

There was a longish pause before the voice said, "Ma'am, the earliest bus leaves at nine-forty A.M."

"Thank you. What does a ticket cost?"

"One way or round trip?"

"Uh — both, please."

"That's eleven sixty-five one way. Eighteen-fifty round trip."

"Thank you."

Wow! Eleven dollars and sixty-five cents was a lot of money for such a short ride. I ran to my room to see if I could manage it.

My cigar box held only six dollars and twelve cents. I found three more pennies in my desk drawer. I needed at least another five dollars and fifty cents just to get there — not to mention getting back.

Getting there was what was important. Reluctantly, I picked up my silver swan. Gram gave the swan bank to me when I was born. Each year she gave me a silver dollar to put inside. There were

146

twelve in it now. There wouldn't be any more. I had planned to keep them forever.

This was no time to be sentimental! I opened the bank and the silver dollars spilled all over my desk. I stuffed all my money in my backpack.

Now came the tricky part. Becca lived too close. I tiptoed to the phone and called Margo.

"Hi, Margo. It's Cindy," I said softly.

"Hi, what's up?"

"I need a favor. A big one. Can you call me back and ask me to spend the day with you tomorrow?"

"Sure. But I thought — "

"Please! Just call. I'll explain later."

"Okay."

I hung up and went back to my room. The phone rang. I waited and let Mom answer it.

"Cindy, it's for you," she called.

"Okay. Thanks," I said and picked up the phone.

"Hi, Cindy," Margo said and waited for the click downstairs. "You're invited to spend the day with me."

I put my hand over the mouthpiece and yelled, "Mom, Margo's invited me to spend Saturday with her."

"That's fine with me," Mom replied. "I don't have anything scheduled."

I sighed with relief. So far, so good. No lies yet, either.

"Thanks, Margo. I'm not coming."

"Huh? What are you up to, Cindy?"

"Listen, Margo. This is real important. I think I know where Jeff is. I'm going to go and get him."

"You are *what?* Why don't you just tell his folks?"

"Because I may be wrong. It would just get their hopes up. Mrs. Johnson can't take much more of that. She's a zombie now. And it'll be okay. I'll be back before anyone knows I've gone." I spoke fast and low. If Margo wouldn't help me I was in big trouble.

Margo hesitated long enough to give me the cold sweats.

"Okay," she finally said. "What time are you *not* coming over?"

I giggled nervously. "About nine-thirty."

"Can't you tell me more?"

"Nope. I'll tell you all about it later. Right now I've got lots of stuff to do."

"Are you sure this is smart, Cindy?"

"I don't know any other way."

"What about your essay?"

"I'll do it Sunday. I won't have time to get it typed now. But I'll write neatly."

"Okay . . . Good luck!"

"Thanks, Margo. You're a real pal."

The tricky part over, I settled down to get ready for my trip. As I remembered, it had only taken a couple of hours, even with several pit stops, for Jeff and me. Still I might need some food. I made several trips downstairs for apples, cookies, and crackers.

148

"That's what happens when you eat your dinner so fast," Mom said on my third trip.

"You're right. I'll try to eat slower next time," I promised.

I set my alarm for eight and crawled into bed at 9:30.

I'm not sure when I went to sleep. I was nervous. What if Jeff had left? Or wasn't there in the first place? What if I couldn't remember the right road? What if they wouldn't sell me a bus ticket. What if? What if?

One hundred little what-ifs standing in a row. One fell over. Ninety-nine to go . . .

I remember the fifty-ninth . . .

16

"What did you do? Rob your piggy bank?"

I gulped and smiled my best smile. I'd picked the woman at the newsstand to change my silver dollars into bills because she looked motherly and nice. "Actually, it was a swan bank. My grandmother gave it to me when I was born. And a silver dollar each year. She said I was to use them for something important."

"And this trip is it?"

"Sure is. I'm going to see my best friend."

"Now, that *is* important. I hope you have a fine visit," the woman said, handing me six crisp one-dollar bills.

"Thank you," I replied. I couldn't bear to part with all of my silver dollars at once. A one-way ticket would have to do.

The next hurdle was buying the ticket. The counter was so high that my eyes could barely peer over the top.

"One way to Laurel Forks, please."

The ticket man looked down and said in a bored voice, "Eleven sixty-five. Gate nine. Bus leaves at nine-forty."

I pushed the money over the counter and he slapped down a ticket. I grabbed it and walked away. My knees were shaking.

"Little girl!"

Shaking? Jelly would look like concrete compared to my legs. Slowly, I turned to face the ticket counter.

The man was smiling. "Your shoes are untied," he said.

I nodded. I couldn't get anything past my closed throat. I bent down and tied the darn shoelaces, then hurried to Gate 9.

I shouldn't have hurried. I sat in the stuffy, smelly bus for fifteen minutes before we finally pulled out.

The bus was only half full. I sat alone by a window for the first half hour or so. At our first stop a fat lady with three shopping bags slopped down beside me. She was a talker.

"Where you going, honey?" she asked first thing.

"To Laurel Forks to see a friend."

"I'm going to see my new grandbaby. He's my fourth. Two boys. Two girls. That's a nice split, isn't it? Of course Selma don't have all four. This is her second. My Joe has the other two. No boys for him yet so I expect he'll keep trying."

She winked at me, fanned herself with a piece of paper, and went on and on . . . and on . . . and on. After she got off at a little place called Trinity, I sat alone again.

The driver seemed to be in no great hurry. He stopped at every little town. The bus began to fill up. When we pulled into a small station in Timberville, he stood up and announced, "Ten-minute rest stop."

I didn't need to rest but I sure needed a bathroom. So did everyone else. I took my place in line and almost missed the bus.

A tall, bony man had my seat when I returned. I saw he had a watch so I asked the time.

"Almost twelve. Want me to put up your pack for you?"

"No, thanks. We'll be in Laurel Forks soon."

"Be about two hours yet."

"Two hours? We've been gone two hours already! It never took this long when we drove in a car."

The man chuckled softly. "Reckon it only takes two hours if you go straight. This is a local bus, honey. Stops for every frog pond and cattle crossing."

He was right. We stopped at places called Emory, Battlecreek, Mt. Clifton, and Briarwood.

The man slept. I ate some cookies and washed them down with an apple. I tried not to think about how late we'd be getting home. Margo was really going to be on the spot — not to mention yours truly.

Finally the driver called out "Laurel Forks."

I made my way quickly up front. "What time do you come back?"

"Monday. Two-thirty or thereabout," he said, opening the door.

I guess my face must have gone all white or something.

"Hey kid. You feel okay?"

I jerked my head up and down.

"I was just kidding. You can get a bus back tomorrow at two-thirty. I don't drive it, though."

"Tomorrow? Two-thirty?"

"That's right."

I swallowed the lump in my throat and got off. The bus pulled away in a cloud of diesel fumes.

Several people were standing around the store. I barely glanced at them. I shouldered my backpack and moved quickly down the road. I sure didn't want to answer a lot of questions about where I was going and why. At the moment I wasn't so sure myself. I knew I was in big trouble even if I found Jeff. Why hadn't I thought to ask about a bus going back? Like a dummy, I'd assumed Trailways ran every hour like our city buses.

153

The turnoff to Laurel Falls was right where I thought it would be; besides, it was well marked. I hiked gradually upward, past the sign marking the National Forest, through thick bushes of budding laurel and on to a rocky, needle-covered trail beside a noisy creek. If I hadn't been so worried I would have enjoyed the walk.

The trail branched off at the foot of the mountain. One trail led to the falls, the other to the cabin. Out of breath, I moved on.

The cabin sat on low stilts a few hundred yards from the creek. It looked deserted. I peered underneath before going up to knock on the door. No one answered.

I jiggled the door. Locked tight. I peeked through a parted window curtain. Everything looked the same as I remembered — rough, heavy furniture in a semicircle before the stone fireplace. I was about to turn away when I saw a gleam of blue. Pressing my forehead against the window, I could just make it out. Jeff's blue gym bag!

My face broke into a wide grin. I was right! Jeff was here.

I dropped my backpack on the porch, cupped my hands, and yelled, "Allie allie in free! Come out, come out wherever you are!"

Silence.

I waited.

Still nothing. I skipped down the steps and walked

around the cabin. The back door was locked, too.

Where could he be? Maybe he was fishing in the pool under the falls. I started up the trail but something made me look back. Jeff's blond head was poking around the outhouse door.

"Jeffrey Stuart Johnson, you come out of there," I yelled.

With a sheepish grin, all of Jeff emerged.

"Hi, Cindy. What are you doing up here?"

"Looking for you, goofy! What else?"

"So? You found me. Anyone else know where I am?"

"Nope. No one else would think of here. Especially since the place isn't your granddad's any more."

Jeff flushed. "Old Colonel Marlow bought it from Gramps. Dad said he never used it. I knew where we kept a key hidden. I banked on it still being there. It was."

"So you just moved in, right? How long did you think you could stay without being found out?"

"Long enough," Jeff answered and stomped toward the house.

I followed him. It was going to be harder than I thought. Evidently Jeff wasn't cold, hungry, or sorry.

Jeff unlocked the door and went inside. "Want a drink? I drew some spring water before you came."

I drank the icy water gratefully.

Jeff went into the front room and flopped on the couch. "I'm not going back," he said. "You can't make me."

"I know that. I came to see if you were all right. Your mom sure isn't."

"What's wrong with Mom? Is she sick or something?"

"Just sick with worry about you is all."

Jeff slumped back on the couch. "She'll get over it."

"I don't think so. She's a basket case. I hardly recognized her yesterday when she was talking — or crying — to Mom. Your whole family has gone bananas. They keep calling the police and the hospitals and running down every rumor anyone tells them."

"Why, for gosh sakes? They'd be better off without me."

"How do you figure that?"

"Because," he mumbled, "you know that trip Mom and Dad have been planning ... to Hawaii? They gave that up just so they could send me to another expensive sports camp! I don't want to go to sports camp ... expensive, cheap, bad or good. I don't want them to give up their dream trip just for me!"

"Did you tell them?"

"NO!"

I knew where he was coming from. There are

156

some things you have a hard time saying to your parents. "So, what are your plans now?"

"I haven't decided yet."

"I guess you'll have to get a job sooner or later," I ventured.

"Yeah, my money won't last long if I have to pay rent, buy food and clothes."

"What kind of job?"

"Maybe a farm job. Maybe in a repair shop. I'm good at fixing things."

I looked Jeff over carefully. "Well, I guess you can get away with it. You look older than you are. They're both good jobs . . . if that's what you want to do with your life."

"It's not!" Jeff exploded. "You know I want to work in electronics, with computers."

"Sure. I know that. I think it's neat. How much do you know about electronics and computers?"

"Not enough," Jeff muttered.

"Aren't there schools where you could learn?"

"Of course there are! You have to have a high school diploma to get in, though."

"Oh, well. You could work and go to school at the same time, couldn't you?"

"I've already thought about that," Jeff said, slumping farther down on the couch. "I don't think so. For one thing, you have to have your past records. My folks would find me, for sure. I guess I'm stuck being a farm hand or a mechanic."

I was losing my patience. Jeff didn't seem to be getting the picture. I stood up and glared at him. "You're not stuck. You're just chicken!"

Jeff jumped up and glared right back at me. "Who are you calling chicken?"

"YOU!" My voice cracked and almost deserted me but I kept going. "You're supposed to be smart. This is dumb. It won't get you what you want. You have to tell your folks how you feel . . . not run off and hide. That's chicken!"

I thought for a minute he was going to sock me. His fists were balled up tight and kept clenching and unclenching. I braced myself and stood my ground.

Finally Jeff turned away. His fists unclenched and his shoulders sagged like an old man's. "Okay. You're right. I'm not going to get what I want this way, either. But I'm *not* chicken. I just didn't want to hurt anyone. Looks like I goofed that too. Let's go catch a bus."

It was my turn to look miserable. "We can't," I said. "There's no bus until tomorrow."

Jeff looked at me and started laughing.

"What's so funny?"

"You!" Jeff guffawed. "You came riding to the rescue and forgot your horse."

"It isn't funny, Jeffrey Stuart!" I shouted. "My folks don't know where I am. Your folks are going crazy. Margo will be in hot water. And I spent my silver dollars . . ." Hot tears began to slide down my cheeks.

Jeff looked panicky. "Hey, don't cry. It's all right. We'll get back."

"How?"

"We'll walk down to Ledbetter's Store and call our folks. They'll come for us."

All of a sudden I wasn't so certain I'd done the right thing. "Are you sure you want to come back? I could go to the store by myself. That would give you time to get away. I can tell your folks that you're okay. That would make your mom feel some better."

"I might as well face the music and get it over with," Jeff mumbled. "Come on, let's get this place straightened up and go."

Jeff was awfully quiet as we cleaned the cabin. I didn't feel much like talking either. I figured there would be plenty of that before the day was over.

"Okay. That's it. The cabin's just like I found it," Jeff said, looking the place over. He locked the door and put the key back in its hiding place.

We walked down the trail in silence, with me taking two steps to Jeff's one.

"You never did tell me how you got here," I said, hoping he'd slow down if he talked.

Jeff grinned. "It was easy. I went to school and homeroom. Then I just walked out and hid in the bread delivery truck. I rode in it all the way to Fenton. I caught a bus from there to Broadview, got some supplies, and walked in."

"How did you know about the bread truck?"

"I've watched it every day for a year. The driver always stays about thirty minutes. Maybe to have a cup of coffee in the cafeteria or something. I figured he served all the schools in our area. I didn't count on him taking me all the way to Fenton. That was pure luck."

"You sure fooled everybody."

"Everybody except you."

"Are you mad?"

Jeff didn't answer right away. He kept on walking, kicking stones out of his way. Then he slowed down for me to catch up and said, "I'm not mad, Cindy, I'm scared."

"You're not the only one."

"Aw, what can they do to us?"

"Send us to reform school," I ventured.

"Feed us bread and water for a month."

"No more movies, TV, or allowances."

"Make me take ballet lessons."

"Make me invite Brandy to spend the weekend."

We thought of wilder and wilder punishments. By the time we reached the store we were laughing like crazy.

There wasn't a pay phone at the store, but Mr. Ledbetter was nice enough to let us use his. I dialed the operator and asked her to reverse the charges.

Mom answered on the first ring. She hardly let the poor operator get her speech out. "Yes! Yes! We'll accept the charges. Cindy? Is that you? Where are you? Are you all right?"

From her panicky voice I knew my story had been blown. "Yes, Mom, I'm fine. I found Jeff."

"Thank God! Where are you?"

"In Ledbetter's Store at Laurel Forks."

"Where?" Mom shouted. Her voice rose two octaves.

"Mr. Johnson knows where it is. It's the place before you get to where his dad had a cabin."

"I know where it is," Dad said on the extension. "Are you and Jeff okay?"

"Sure. We're fine. I just didn't know about bus schedules. I thought Trailways ran every hour like the Metro. We can't get a bus until tomorrow."

"Tomorrow?" Mom screeched. "You stay right where you are. We'll come get you."

"Okay."

"We'll call the Johnsons and be on our way," Dad said. "Stay put!"

"Uh — Dad, could you and Mom come for me? I think Jeff needs to talk to his folks without anyone around."

"And we need to talk to you!" Mom said ominously.

"We'll come for you," Dad said.

"Thanks."

Jeff was standing beside me, shifting from one foot to the other. "She knows, huh?"

"Yeah. I don't know how she found out that I wasn't at Margo's."

"Now both of you are in trouble because of me," Jeff said.

I gave Jeff one of my pluckiest grins. "Don't look so glum, chum. I've been in hot water before. In fact, it's my natural habitat, if you remember."

Mr. Ledbetter had been listening to our conversation. He couldn't help it since the phone was next to the counter. "You kids hungry? I was about to heat me a snack. Could I interest you in a sandwich or something?" he asked.

"I'm not hungry. Thanks," Jeff replied.

"Well, I am," I said. The apple and cookies I'd eaten on the bus had run out long ago. The mere thought of food caused a hollow feeling in my stomach.

Mr. Ledbetter heated three sandwiches in his microwave — which was pretty smart because Jeff changed his mind.

We took our food out to the front steps of the store and ate. Mr. Ledbetter stayed right with us even after he closed the store. I think he was afraid we might decide to run away again. Two hours seemed to go by awfully fast.

Jeff's face turned two shades paler when he saw two cars come roaring down the road.

162

Mrs. Johnson was out of her car before it stopped. She ran to Jeff and hugged him.

"I don't know whether to hug you or hit you," Dad said as he and Mom tried to hug me at the same time.

When I could get loose, I said, "I'm sorry. I didn't mean to cause any trouble."

Mom sighed and shook her head. "Well, you certainly did. For us and Margo."

I really felt bad about Margo. "How'd you find out I wasn't at Margo's?" I asked.

Dad squeezed my shoulder. "Get in the car, honey. We'll talk about it."

Mrs. Johnson came over and got mushy all over me. I didn't know what to say so I didn't say anything.

When we were finally on our way, Mom said, "All right, Cindy. How did you know where to find Jeff?"

"It's a long story. I didn't at first. Then I saw my bath powder. Somehow I just knew Jeff was here. But I didn't have any proof. Dad said to get my facts straight before I spoke. The only way I knew how to get the facts was to come and see for myself. Mrs. Johnson said she couldn't take any more false hopes."

"I think I understand most of that — except for the bath powder," Dad said with a chuckle.

"You said you were spending the day with Margo.

That's the first time I've ever known you to lie to me," Mom said sadly.

"I didn't lie," I protested. "Margo did ask me to spend the day. All I did was repeat what Margo said. I never asked to go or said I was."

Mom shook her head. "Cindy, you know better. Maybe you didn't tell me an outright lie, but you deliberately misled me, which is just as bad."

"I'm sorry, Mom. I didn't know any other way to do it. It would have worked if the bus schedule had been right. How *did* you find out I wasn't at Margo's?"

"I ran into Mrs. Wagner in the grocery store. I asked what you and Margo were doing. Mrs. Wagner looked puzzled. She said, 'Margo and I are doing the weekly baking. Cindy isn't at our house.' Well, you can imagine how I felt! Or can you? Anyway, I went home with Mrs. Wagner and that's when I found out about your rescue mission — although Margo didn't know very much."

"You put your friend in an awkward position, Cindy," Dad said. "Though this time I think I understand your reason."

Mom shot him a hard look. "Speaking of reasons, why did Jeff run away?"

I didn't think Jeff would mind, under the circumstances, so I told them.

"That's really too bad," Dad said when I finished. "How did you know all this?"

"I understand Jeff 'cause he's a misfit in his family

164

just like I am," I replied honestly. "Except I don't mind as much."

"What do you mean? You're not a misfit," Mom exclaimed.

"Oh, come on, Mom. I'm not pretty and popular like Ellen or smart and together like Grace. I'll never be a Sweetheart of Sigma Chi or a Frankenheim scholar. I couldn't even get the job of class reporter."

"Cindy, you're not being fair to yourself," Mom said. "Your sisters are much older."

"Hah! They never got into the messes I get into even when they were my age, did they?"

I had Mom there. She was too stunned to answer.

Dad was laughing. "Maybe not. But I'll tell you something, Cindy. You're the most interesting child we have. Don't sell yourself short."

"What does that mean? I *am* short!"

When Mom stopped laughing she said, "It means we love you just the way you are, escapades and all. Give yourself some time to excel. You already fit into our family just fine."

Who can understand parents? One minute they're fussing at you, the next they are giggling like a couple of little kids!

"Speaking of fits," Dad said, "I'm going to throw a dandy one if we don't get something to eat soon. My stomach thinks that my throat has been cut."

"I don't doubt it," Mom said. "You didn't have any dinner."

"Neither did you," Dad replied.

"We had hot ham and cheese sandwiches, Cokes, and fresh roasted peanuts," I said smugly.

"Quiet, Calamity Jane! Or I'll stop the car and roast you over an open fire," Dad threatened.

Instead we found a Burger Barn and had dinner.

The first thing I did when I got home was call Margo to apologize. And you know what? She wasn't even mad!

"What are friends for?" she said. "I'm glad you're back safe and that you found Jeff and got him to come home." She paused then giggled. "I think he's kind of cute."

Jeff? I hadn't thought about him that way.

"Yeah," I said after a pause. "He is."

Becca came over in a mixed mood. She was glad we were back, but pretty hacked because I hadn't included her in my plans.

I explained how I couldn't have used her because she lived too close and Mom could have checked on me too easily.

"Well, the next time you and Jeff go adventuring, don't forget me. After all, I'm the third member of the Three Mosquitoes!" Becca said.

"Gosh," I exclaimed, laughing, "I haven't thought about that in ages!"

Together we chanted:

> "Float like a butterfly.
> Bite like a flea.
> Who's the greatest?
> The Mosquitoes Three!"

"Remember we signed in blood. I think that makes it count no matter how old we get or how many other friends we have," Becca said seriously.

"You're right," I said with a happy, warm feeling in my chest. "I won't ever forget that again."

Sunday I wrote my essay. This time the words flowed easily from my head onto the paper.

17

"It's going to be okay," Jeff said, giving me a thumbs-up sign at the bus stop Monday morning. "Dad says we may even get a computer!"

"That's great!"

Jeff grinned all over his face. "The greatest part is that I don't ever have to go to a sports camp again."

"How about the computer camp?"

"Hey now, I didn't want to push my luck. What about you? Were your folks pretty sore?"

"Not really. I got a lecture on telling the truth — and nothing but the truth. For some reason, they were glad to have me back."

"That figures. Their lives would be pretty dull without you around," Jeff said. "They never know what Calamity Jane will do next."

For once that name didn't make me flinch inside. I

guess if my folks could love me, escapades and all, I could accept myself for what I was.

Under Brandy's smirking gaze, I turned in my essay.

"I suppose you were too busy to get yours typed," she said after class. "I heard about you running away to be with Jeff Johnson."

The last part was said loudly, so everyone in the hall could hear it.

"Watch your mouth, girl!" Andrea said, pushing Brandy against her locker.

"I'm only telling the truth," Brandy whimpered.

Right then I understood what Mom meant by being misleading even though you were truthful. "That's okay, Andrea," I said calmly. "She's right, but it wasn't like she tried to make it sound."

"It is *not* okay," Becca retorted. "It was mean and nasty."

"You take that back!" Brandy said. "Or you can tear up your invitation to my party!"

"Who cares?" Becca snapped. "Come on, Cindy. Let's get some fresh air. Something smells around here."

We walked away, leaving Brandy gawking.

To tell the truth, I was gawking too. I hadn't expected Becca's outburst. Then I began smiling. When you're on a lucky roll, don't knock it.

I thought my luck had run out when I was called to the principal's office Thursday morning.

169

With slow steps and racing thoughts, I went to the office. I couldn't think of one thing I had done wrong. I'd taken all my showers. I hadn't been tardy once. In fact I'd been on my best behavior for weeks. I'd even helped with the orientation tours . . .

"Mr. Zale is expecting you," Mrs. Anderson said. "Go right in."

Mr. Zale was waiting for me, hands folded on his desk. "Good morning, Cindy. I understand you were one of our tour guides yesterday."

"Yes, sir."

"Just what kind of tour did you give our prospective students?"

My heart sank to its familiar resting place in the pit of my stomach. Sheeze! I'd forgotten my own first rule: Adults don't have the same sense of humor as kids. "Uh — just the usual tour," I hedged. "You said to prepare them."

Mr. Zale passed his hand over his face. "Listen to this message I found on my answering machine this morning, please."

". . . Mr. Zale, this is Laura Baughman. I'm a sixth grade teacher at Peavy Elementary School. I want to compliment you on your choice of guides for orientation — at least the one our group had. Cindy put our students at ease. The imitations she did were priceless. You should have all of your guides so relaxed and informative. My group came back eager to attend Ruffner next fall. I can assure you that isn't always the case . . ."

170

Mr. Zale clicked off the machine. His eyes were twinkling even though his face was serious. "Cindy, a good administrator should know what he is doing right as well as what he is doing wrong. So, tell me. What did you do?"

I could feel my face going all red. "Nothing much. I took them around to all the important places — the library, the gym, the cafeteria. I guess I might have mentioned some of the surprises I had last year."

"Such as?"

"Taking showers with fifty other girls. Getting used to six teachers. Lockers that won't open and shut. Which restrooms to use. Stuff like that."

"And the imitations?"

"Well, I sort of gave them a rundown on their teachers. You know, it's kind of scary to have six teachers to figure out all at once. So I told them a little about each teacher. I wasn't mean or anything."

"I see," Mr. Zale said, smiling all over his face. "Well, next year I'll certainly consult with you before orientation. Maybe we can improve our techniques. Thank you for this information, Cindy. You may go back to your class now."

He was chuckling when I left. I wasn't. I felt fortunate that my mouth hadn't gotten me in more trouble.

I hurried back to math class. We were reviewing for our final exams. Since I'd begun asking Miss

Kilper for help when I needed it my math grades had improved. I still had to work my tail off. But, if I made a B on the exams, I'd have a B average for the year. I planned to study all weekend.

So when Becca called and asked me to her slumber party I said, "Sorry, Becca. I'd love to come, but I'm going to study all weekend. I'm going to make a B on that exam if it kills me."

"You have to come, Cindy," Becca wailed. "It won't be any fun without you. All the girls who aren't going to Brandy's party are coming."

"Sorry, Becca," I said, cutting her off. I was afraid if she kept talking I'd give in. "Work before pleasure this time. You all have fun."

I hung up and saw Mom staring at me. "I think you should go to Becca's party," she said.

Now it was my turn to stare. "Hey, you're always on my case about my grades! Now you want me to go to a party instead of studying?"

Mom smiled. "All work and no play will make Cindy a dull girl. Besides, you've been working very hard in school and in band. You deserve a break. Call Becca back and say you'll go to her party."

"But my math — "

"You can review Friday night and Sunday afternoon. If you don't know the material after that, cramming won't help. Call Becca."

Who can figure parents? I called Becca right away.

Surprisingly, four of the Secret Circle girls came

to Becca's. It seems their parents heard that Mr. and Mrs. Wine would be out of town and they wouldn't let their daughters attend an unchaperoned party.

"My parents treat me like a baby," Gina Harris complained. "Twelve-year-olds don't need chaperones!"

"Your parents can't be as bad as mine," Della Dandridge scoffed. "My dad would be happy if I wore hoop skirts and blouses buttoned up to my neck."

"Ha! Hoop skirts are modern frills to my parents," Margo said. "I can't have a date until I'm sixteen. And then they have to meet the boy and approve of him."

Margo's remark triggered an awesome gripe session. We didn't get much slumbering done at the slumber party, but we had a great time. (Of course, I'm not speaking for Dr. and Mrs. Morgan. They looked more bleary-eyed than we did on Sunday morning.)

I went home and sacked out until Mom woke me up for lunch. I ate and went straight to my room to study. That's when the phone calls began.

Everyone wanted to tell me about Brandy's party. She sure knew how to throw a super bash! The pool party had games and relay races with prizes for the winners. The picnic wasn't your ordinary picnic, either. It was a Hawaiian luau. Catered, no less! They even had the Freak-Outs, our area's most popular band, to listen and dance to for the whole evening.

Everything was cool until later in the party when the band took a break. It seems they located Mr. Wine's liquor stash and helped themselves. They weren't selfish, either. They shared. Depending on who was telling the story, (a) only the band members got bombed, (b) only some of the guys did, (c) everyone (except the caller) did.

There weren't any party-crashers, but there was plenty of excitement without them — when the parents came to pick up their kids.

No one wore their gold circles to school Monday morning.

Brandy was unusually quiet. I felt kind of sorry for her. It wasn't her fault if the Freak-Outs lived up to their name.

Mom was right. Again. Taking a little time off didn't seem to hurt my exams any. I wasn't even the last one to finish in math. Miss Kilper looked pleased when I handed in my paper before the bell rang.

Before I knew it, it was Honors Night. Mom and Dad were coming to my last concert. I was nervous and a little sad. This would be Garth's final time with our band. One piece we were playing featured the sax section. I sure hoped I didn't goof up his last effort.

"Do I look okay?" I asked, adjusting my concert jacket.

"You look wonderful," Mom said. (Moms are like that. It would have been the same if I'd had on a potato sack.)

"Even your shoes are tied," Dad said, looking down at my shiny black oxfords.

I stuck out my tongue at him. "Okay, I'm ready. I'll have to take my other clothes to change into. We have to turn in our uniforms tonight."

"I have them. Let's go or we'll never find a parking place," Mom said.

She was right. The parking lot and all the side streets were full of cars. Honors Night is a big deal at Ruffner. It's kind of a mini-graduation for ninth graders, awards night, and band concert all rolled into one evening.

I peeked out from behind the curtain when we took our concert chairs. The auditorium was full. I saw Brandy and her parents sitting in the first row at one side. She looked beautiful — calm and confident.

I didn't have time to worry about Brandy as the curtain rose and everyone stood while the ninth graders marched in. When everyone was seated, the ninth grade band members came up on stage.

Mr. Zale welcomed everyone and gave a short speech.

We played two selections.

Mr. Zale gave out some awards.

We played another piece.

175

More awards.

We played our next to last selection, the one featuring the saxes. (I thought this one got louder applause.)

Mr. Zale came to the microphone again. "Our last award is a new one. This year the Literary Guild is sponsoring a creative writing contest. First place winners will receive twenty-five dollars; second place, fifteen; and third place, ten. In addition the first place winners will have their work entered in the state creative writing contest. Our local judges were Dr. Sandra Kaufman, Mr. Ellis Tillet, and Dr. Frank Merritt. I am pleased to introduce Dr. Merritt, who will present these awards."

"Thank you, Mr. Zale. It is indeed a pleasure to be presenting these awards to seventh, eighth, and ninth graders. It gives me hope for the future. I teach freshman English at Maymount College and you have no idea how many college freshmen can't write a complete sentence, much less an essay, poem, or short story. Not so with these young people. Their work is excellent and your teachers are to be commended. However, I'm sure some of the credit goes to the parents as well. You have supported and assisted their endeavors. I congratulate all of you.

"Since we are honoring our ninth grade students tonight I will begin with them . . ."

The names and the applause went on and on — like slow motion or a dream. My palms were sweaty. My mouth was dry.

". . . First place in essay, Cynthia Jane Cunningham for her essay entitled 'Friendship.' "

I heard him but it took two nudges from Kelly to get me to my feet. Even then I couldn't seem to move. Kelly gave me a gentle shove.

I pitched forward — right over our music stand. Sheet music flew everywhere. I looked on helplessly as other band members scampered after them.

The audience was laughing. Someone yelled, "Did you trip over your shoelaces, Cindy?"

That unfroze me. I looked down at my neatly tied shoes and laughed. I moved to the microphone. "Not this time," I said. "This time I *almost* got everything right."

"You certainly did this essay right," Dr. Merritt said, presenting me with the check. "Congratulations."

I shook his hand and moved back to my chair in a daze. I'd done it! Me, Cynthia Jane Cunningham. I'd actually done something of real value.

I don't remember playing our last piece, but I guess I did.

When the curtains closed, everyone gathered around to congratulate me. Garth was last.

"Way to go, Cindy!" he said. "I didn't know you were a writer as well as a musician."

"Neither did I."

Garth twiddled with his glasses. "Oh — how about going out to celebrate after we change? My brother can drop us off at High's."

He said it so fast I almost didn't catch it. "Huh? Oh, yeah. Sure!" I answered. "Let me change and tell my folks."

Garth let his breath out in a whoosh. "Okay. I'll bet they're proud of you. I'll meet you at the side door."

I nodded and ran to change. Everything seemed to take twice as long. It always does when you are in a hurry.

The halls were still crowded when I finally got dressed and went to meet my folks. Margo, Becca, Andrea, and a bunch of other people hugged and congratulated me as I struggled toward the trophy case where I could see Mom and Dad.

The glow of pride in their eyes was worth more than any prize or check could ever be. And this time it was for me.

Mom hugged me so tight I could hardly breathe. "You never even told us you were entering the contest! We thought we were coming just to your concert! We're very proud of you, Cindy."

Dad's eyes were twinkling. "I'll say! Of course, this isn't the first time you've surprised us. I'm sure it's not the last."

"Of course it isn't," I assured him. "What would life be without surprises?"

"Dull," Dad answered promptly.

Guess who came up then? Brandy and her parents! Mrs. Wine gave me such syrupy congratulations that

I almost choked. You could tell she didn't mean one word of all that goo.

Brandy smiled and sweet things came out of her mouth, but her eyes said "Just you wait!"

"Thank you," I said politely. My eyes accepted her challenge.

"I hope you keep on with your writing, Cindy," Miss Carpenter said, giving me a hug. "Your ideas on friendship show maturity far beyond your years. I enjoyed having you in my class this year."

That's when it hit me. The first year of middle school was over. I had survived!

"Are you ready to go home now?" Dad asked.

"Uh — yes — well, no, not exactly. Garth wants me to go celebrate at High's. Is that okay?"

Mom smiled a funny little smile. "Certainly. You go right along. We'll see you later."

Dad looked puzzled. "Who's this Garth?"

Mom patted his arm. "Never mind, James. Don't be late, Cindy."

I took off. I hoped Garth was still waiting. It seemed like I'd been in that hall for ages.

Garth, Colin, and Colin's girlfriend Sue were waiting by the side door. No one said very much on the ride to High's. Colin let us off and drove away. High school kids don't hang out at High's.

It felt different being at High's with Garth. I don't know how to explain it. The same kids were there. The place looked the same. And the Triple Delight was just as yummy and gooey as ever. But it *was* different somehow.

Garth and I didn't have any trouble finding things to talk about. In fact, we yakked all the way home — the whole eight blocks.

"You are going to band camp, aren't you?" Garth asked as we started up the steps at my house.

"Sure! I wouldn't miss it for anything."

"Good. Then we'll get to be together this summer. In band, I mean. The high school and middle school bands camp together."

"We're sure going to miss you at Ruffner next year," I said sadly. "Band won't be the same."

"You won't miss me. You'll take first chair. You'll do fine."

"Me? What about Kelly?"

"You're better than she is any day. I'll bet you money you'll take first."

"You're on!" I stuck out my hand to shake on the deal.

Instead, Garth leaned down and kissed me. Right on the lips!

Then he took off like an Olympic sprinter. "Night," he yelled from halfway down the drive.

I waved feebly. My lips felt funny. In fact I felt funny all over.

"Is that you, Cindy?" Mom called. "You and Garth come in and have a Coke."

I floated into the house. Boy, this had been some day!

"He's gone," I said, smiling at Mom and Dad. "It's been a long day."

"And a good one," Mom said happily. "Let's call Ellen and Grace with the good news."

I giggled. "It's Friday night, Mom. Grace and Ellen won't be in the dorms! I'll call first thing in the morning."

"If you don't, I will," Mom said. "They'll be just as proud of you as we are."

"Are you going to let us read that prize-winning essay sometime?" Dad asked.

"I sure am," I promised. I kissed them both and retreated to my room. I had lots and lots to think about . . . middle school . . . the contest . . . band . . . Garth . . .

The best thing about middle school, I think, is the friends I've made. The first line of my essay floated in my head: "Friends come in all sizes, shapes, and sexes." It's true. That's why an essay on friendship was easy to write.

The good things in band were just beginning. We would get better and better. Playing music together is very satisfying.

There are other things that are very satisfying, too . . .

Thinking of Garth's kiss, I pulled out my journal and wrote:

RULE NO. *10: Never say* never.